WORKOUT WISHES & VALENTINE KISSES

THE WISHING TREE SERIES, BOOK 5

BARBARA HINSKE

PRAISE FOR BARBARA HINSKE

Know an author who can grab you on the very first page so that you HAVE to keep reading? If not, then you must read Barbara Hinske. –Amazon Reviewer

Barbara Hinske writes the most engaging stories that you just cannot put down. –Amazon Reviewer

Barbara Hinske always introduces characters that become your friends and sets her novels so that you are immediately drawn in and your interest is held to the end, which is always neatly tied together, often in a surprising and unexpected way. –Amazon Reviewer

Barbara Hinske has written another warm and gentle book about people who care. The story reminds the reader that the world is full of love and compassion.... –Amazon Reviewer

You will feel uplifted and refreshed. –Amazon Reviewer

Workout Wishes & Valentine Kisses
by Barbara Hinske

ISBN: 978-1-7349249-5-4

LCCN: 2021917380

Casa del Northern Publishing

Phoenix, Arizona

For our wonderful readers in My Book Friends.

ALSO BY BARBARA HINSKE

The Rosemont Series

Coming to Rosemont

Weaving the Strands

Uncovering Secrets

Drawing Close

Bringing Them Home

Shelving Doubts

Restoring What Was Lost

No Matter How Far

Novellas

The Night Train

The Christmas Club (adapted for The Hallmark Channel, 2019)

Paws and Pastries

Novels in the Emily Series

Guiding Emily

The Unexpected Path

Novels in the "Who's There?!" Collection

CHAPTER 1

*P*am Olson wove her way through the boisterous Friday night crowd at Woody's Pizza to the takeout window at the far corner of the bar.

"Hey, Pam. It's been a while." The older gentleman working the register had been there for years.

"As a personal trainer, I need to look fit and healthy," the athletic brunette replied, "so I watch what I eat. But I've had such a long week, I decided I needed to treat myself."

The man chuckled. "Glad to hear it. You haven't got an ounce of fat on you, from what I can tell. Sometimes, you just need to eat pizza." He checked the stack of boxes to his left. "Your order isn't up yet. Sorry about that—we've been slammed. Shouldn't be more than another ten minutes."

"I'll wait over there," she said, pointing to a spot

along the wall. All she wanted to do was get her pizza and go home. She'd kick off her athletic shoes, turn on HGTV, and snuggle with Leopold while she ate and looked for DIY design inspiration from her favorite network.

She scanned the people congregated at the bar or leaning against small, high-topped tables. It was hard to believe that she'd been one of these high-spirited college students only ten years ago. The noise level was almost deafening. Everyone was jovial—and no one, other than herself, was alone.

She checked her watch, anxious to get away from this stark reminder of her current circumstance. It had only been two minutes since she'd stepped away from the counter. Eight more to go.

She resumed people-watching when a tall man with his back to her at a table in the far corner turned his head enough for her to see his profile. Her stomach dropped to her knees. It couldn't be. Boston was over a hundred and thirty miles away. He wouldn't be in Linden Falls. She'd had to put her foot down and insist that they visit her mother here—and even then, he often backed out at the last minute, leaving her to make the trip on her own. What had he always called this place? *A hick town where everyone acts like they're on a maple syrup sugar high.* She'd always hated that. The people of Linden Falls were kind and happy. He was just too cynical to see it.

Pam inhaled sharply and strained to observe the man. Dark, wavy hair hit his shirt collar and turned up in a way that was all too familiar. It was him, all right. Lance Foster—her ex-husband—was in Linden Falls. She pressed her back against the wall as she continued to stare at him.

The hostess approached a group milling around in front of Lance. When they moved away, following the hostess to their table, her view was suddenly unobstructed.

Lance sat across from a well-endowed woman with unnaturally blond hair and overdone makeup. She leaned toward him, laughing, as the revealing V-neck of her sweater gaped open. Pam knew exactly what the woman was doing—she'd seen her do the same thing countless times before. Connie Sexton—their Boston next-door neighbor—was here, in Linden Falls, with Lance.

Connie had flirted with Lance every chance she got. She always managed to come out the door when Lance was working in the yard or stop over to borrow something when Pam wasn't home. When she'd first mentioned her irritation with Connie to Lance, he'd dismissed her concerns. As time wore on, they'd quarreled over Connie's intentions, and Lance had derided Pam's suspicions.

Pam pulled her dark chestnut ponytail out of the collar of her jacket. The back of her neck was damp with perspiration. She had been right. Lance and Connie were an item and had probably been having an affair—right under her nose.

She watched as Lance ran his finger up Connie's

arm and along her jawline, stopping at her lips. Then he leaned in and kissed her in an intimate fashion.

The packed restaurant suddenly felt claustrophobic. Pam's vision was hazy, and she blinked rapidly to clear her unwanted tears. To hell with her pizza. She turned on her heel and pushed her way through the door marked Emergency Exit.

The early-fall night air stung her damp cheeks. She stood, crying softly, and took deep breaths to steady herself.

The emergency door opened behind her, and the man from behind the bar walked to her, a pizza box in his outstretched hand.

"I'm…I'm sorry," she stammered as she thrust her hand into her purse, looking for her wallet.

The man touched her elbow. "This one's on the house."

"No…you can't… I've got my wallet in here somewhere."

"I saw you duck out. I also think I know why." His voice was kind. "I've seen a lot of things, working in that bar my whole life. Some good, some not so good. I think you could do with a little bit of kindness, and a pizza is all I have to offer."

"Thank you." She choked on the words as she took the box from him.

He began to retrace his steps. "Drive careful getting home. Whoever he is, he's not worth getting in a wreck over."

Pam nodded as the delicious aroma of the pizza caused her stomach to gurgle. The man was right. Lance Foster wasn't worth one more moment of her time.

CHAPTER 2

*P*am groaned as she raised a hand to deflect the cat paw tapping at her cheek. "Leopold," she said, drawing out his name as she spoke. She brought her other hand to the large calico cat who had adopted her the day she had moved back to town more than a year ago. Cupping her hands under his chest, she maneuvered him off of her.

Leopold emitted a short retort that conveyed his displeasure and hopped from the sofa to the rug.

Pam swung her feet to the floor and pushed herself into a sitting position. She brushed a strand of hair out of her eyes that had escaped the ponytail, now hanging limply at the nape of her neck. When was the last time she'd fallen asleep in front of the television and spent the night on her sofa?

She snatched the remote from the coffee table and switched off the program currently playing. She'd already seen it—the couple was going to love it and not list it.

The pizza box lay open—and empty—in front of her. She'd eaten the whole thing, drowning her sorrow at seeing her ex and his girlfriend in a carbohydrate overload.

Pam forced herself to her feet and shuffled to the kitchen, Leopold impeding her progress by weaving between her legs. She stuffed the stale-smelling box into the trash and started as she noted the time. She was going to be late.

In one swift motion, she filled Leopold's dish with his kibble and set it on the heart-shaped mat on the floor. She looked longingly at her fancy French press coffeepot but told herself she didn't have time—she'd grab a cup when she got to the farmers' market. She didn't even have time for a shower. She'd splash some water on her face, change her clothes, and head out the door. She could brush her hair and redo her ponytail in the car. Helping her mother, Irene, sell her homemade aprons and table linens at her booth at the market didn't require Pam to look her best.

She shot out of her backdoor ten minutes later, hairbrush held between her teeth, and raced down the steps to the driveway and her Prius. The town square was only minutes away, but by the time she got there, it was already surrounded by parked cars or people looking for a place to park. The Saturday morning market, boasting more than a hundred produce, food, and craft vendors, was popular with both locals and tourists—especially during the fall, when carloads of leaf peepers invaded the area.

She made a quick U-turn and headed for her dentist's office, one block off the square. Her dentist didn't mind if Pam parked in her lot on the weekends when the office was closed. Pam parked her Prius, took three swipes through her hair with her brush, and secured her ponytail in an elastic band. She tossed her brush onto the passenger seat, locked the car, and set off for her mother's booth at a fast jog.

The market didn't officially open for another twenty minutes, but the volume of people heading for the square indicated they'd have a busy day in front of them. Pam hoped so. Her mother worked so hard, sewing late into the night, five days a week, to create the cheerful table linens and aprons she was famous for.

Irene was chatting with a customer while she attempted to set up her display of aprons when Pam breezed into the booth. She smiled as Pam took the box Irene was unpacking.

"Good morning," Pam said, greeting her mother as well as a woman examining a set of quilted placemats with a coordinating table runner. "I'll finish setting up," she told Irene. "I'm sorry I'm late."

"Nonsense. You're right on time."

"Leave the rest of this to me." Pam cut her eyes toward the customer. "Maybe she has some questions."

Irene mouthed the words *thank you* as she brushed a strand of her silver bob off of her face and turned toward the shopper. "Are you looking for any particular color or style?"

The woman looked up from the display. "These are all so pretty. I love the vibrant colors. I can't decide between these two patterns," she said, picking up two sets from the long table stacked with table linens.

Irene pointed to the sign that said, "Buy One, Get One Half Off."

"Really? That's awesome. I'll take both of these," the woman said, handing the two sets to Irene.

Pam caught Irene's eye and nodded approvingly.

"Have you seen our seasonal selections? We've got fall-themed table lines over here"—Irene motioned toward a table at the front of the booth—"and we've got Christmas items in the back."

"I love anything with pumpkins and fall leaves," the woman replied. "Can you hang on to these for me while I take a look?"

Pam took the items from Irene. "I'll put them in the back corner," she said as the woman approached the fall display that Pam had just neatly arranged. Irene asked the woman if she would be hosting Thanksgiving, and she and her customer were soon chatting about holiday entertaining as the woman riffled through the inventory. Pam sighed. At least half of her day would be spent straightening displays.

A familiar voice nearby drew Pam's attention. Neva Cabot, the owner of the venerable Wishing Tree Inn, was extolling the virtues of the local, herbal-infused honeys sold by their neighbor in the next booth. Pam eavesdropped for a moment.

"I came to the market because I felt an urgent need for lavender honey," said Neva, who went on to explain the soothing properties of sage honey for a sore throat and the relaxing properties of chamomile honey. Pam made a mental note to pick up a jar of the chamomile honey before she left that day.

Pam turned her attention back to her mother's booth when the customer touched her arm and handed her two holiday aprons and an additional set of place-mats. "Can you add these to the placemat sets I gave you? I think this had better be it for me."

"Of course," Pam said, retrieving the other items the woman had selected. "I can help you with all of this."

Irene remained at the front of her booth, greeting shoppers as they passed by.

Pam was bent over her calculator, adding the total and filling out a sales slip, when the sudden change in the tone of her mother's voice caught her attention. She looked up in time to see Lance—with Connie glued to his side—making small talk with her mother.

A wave of panic washed over Pam—just like it had when she'd seen them the night before—but at least this time, it didn't puddle at her feet, feeling like it was going to suck her under. She swallowed hard. Lance would know that she would be helping her mother in the booth. He had come here, on purpose, to show her that he was with Connie. Lance Foster was doing what he excelled at—hurting people, making them feel "less than." All to make himself feel better than everyone else.

"Are you all right, dear?" the woman asked, bending over to peer up into Pam's face. "You look like you've seen a ghost."

"I'm fine. Absolutely fine." Pam forced her attention back to her calculator. "Your total, with tax, is one hundred eighty-five dollars."

The woman offered Pam her credit card. Pam processed the payment and handed the card and her packages to the woman. "Please come see us when you're in Linden Falls again." She gave the woman a business card. "Call us with any questions. If you'd like additional items, we've got an online store on our website, and shipping is always free."

"That's terrific."

"Thank you for shopping with us. Enjoy the rest of your day." Pam took a deep breath and squared her shoulders before joining her mother at the front of the booth.

"I thought that was you," Lance said with exaggerated civility.

"That ponytail of yours, well, it never changes, does it?" Connie asked rhetorically, a sweet smile on her lips that didn't match the bitchy tone of her voice. "You still sport that just-rolled-out-of-bed look."

Pam felt the muscles in her shoulders tighten. Darn it—the odious woman was right. She had just rolled out of bed. "What are you doing here?"

"We're looking at a horse over at the stables on the

outskirts of town. Connie's thinking of buying him for her daughter."

Pam crossed her arms over her chest and stood in silence.

Irene placed her hand on Pam's waist as she glowered at the man who had broken her daughter's heart. "You're a long way from the stables. Can I help you with something?"

"No…we had some time to kill before our appointment there this morning and thought we'd stop by to say hello."

Connie pressed Lance's arm against the curve of her body and smiled coyly at Pam and Irene.

A woman wheeled a sleeping baby in a stroller up to the front table. "Excuse me," she said, maneuvering the stroller and causing Lance and Connie to step aside. "I've been looking for your booth. My mom loves your stuff, and I want to get her Christmas present."

Irene began to assist the young mother as another customer entered the booth.

"Don't let us keep you," Pam said, narrowing her eyes at Lance. If he thought he was going to upset her, make her jealous, he was seriously mistaken. Seeing him with Connie had startled her last night and opened old wounds, but she wasn't going to give either of them the satisfaction of seeing her upset.

Connie emitted an exaggerated sigh before Lance led her away from the booth.

Irene and Pam were both occupied with a deluge of customers for the next several hours. By midafternoon, the skies had darkened, and rain was imminent. The remaining customers were all completing their purchases before dashing to their cars.

"I think that's it for today," Irene said. "Let's get packed up before it all gets soaked."

Pam and Irene worked seamlessly, in practiced fashion, and had what little merchandise had not sold boxed up in under ten minutes. They collapsed the booth and transported everything to Irene's SUV on a large rolling cart. They were just finishing loading the car when the first fat raindrop hit the windshield. The drop was followed by another and then another, prompting the two to dive into the car for refuge.

"Do you mind giving me a lift to my car?" Pam asked.

"Of course not," Irene said. "We haven't had a second to talk about the bizarre appearance of Lance with that dreadful woman."

"It was crazy, wasn't it?"

"Completely. The man who hates Linden Falls…is suddenly here?" She turned in her seat to look at Pam. "You handled that with such composure, honey. I was so proud of you. I would have fallen apart."

"I'd seen them already."

Irene raised her eyebrows.

"I picked up a pizza at Woody's last night, and I spotted them at a table. That woman he was with— she's our former next-door neighbor."

"The one you thought he was having an affair with? Which he denied."

Pam nodded. "I guess I was right, after all."

"Did you talk to them?"

"No. I ran out of Woody's like someone was chasing me. It threw me for a loop."

"Why didn't you call me?"

"I don't know. I was so raw; I didn't want to talk about it right then. I figured I'd tell you this morning. And then I overslept and got to the booth late, and we were slammed with customers."

"He figured you'd be helping me at the booth. He was trying to make you jealous—trying to hurt you." Irene's tone hardened. "What a complete ass he is!"

"That's what I think—on all counts," Pam said.

"As I said, you handled it perfectly. He didn't get what he came for, that's for sure. As I said, I'm proud of you."

"Thanks, Mom."

"Let's treat ourselves. I know just where to go," Irene said, starting her engine.

"The Wishing Tree Inn?"

"Where else? We both could do with a cup of Neva's tea."

"Sweetened with some of that infused honey?"

"Exactly. We'll also need her pumpkin spice scones. My mouth is watering already. If we're lucky, maybe Neva will have time to sit with us and have a cup herself."

"She helped you cope when Dad died, didn't she?"

Irene nodded. "I don't know what I would have done without her."

"I'm glad I moved back," Pam said. "Linden Falls is a special place." She glanced at her mother. "And I'm not talking about that silly Wishing Tree. You know I don't believe in all of that nonsense. The people here—like Neva—are what make it wonderful."

Irene nodded and kept her eyes on the road. Maybe Pam didn't believe in the magic of the Wishing Tree, but she knew better.

CHAPTER 3

*N*eva Cabot set the plate of fresh-out-of-the-oven scones on the small round table tucked into a corner by the window. The fragrant aromas of pumpkin and spices wafted upward with the steam escaping from the delectable pastries. Two middle-aged women—sisters by the looks of them—settled back into their overstuffed chairs.

"These look amazing. I'm glad it rained, forcing us to leave the market early," said one of the women while the other broke off a piece of scone and popped it into her mouth.

"OMG!" the woman groaned and covered her mouth with her hand. "You wouldn't find anything better in Boston."

Neva's spine stiffened, but she kept a smile plastered on her face. Why in the world did people think that small towns couldn't possibly keep up with big cities? "Thank you," she said as she brought her eyes up to the window and noticed the familiar SUV with its two female passengers pull to the curb across from the Wishing Tree Inn. "Enjoy," she said and crossed to the front door.

Neva flung open the door of the inn she'd owned and managed for more than forty years. She stood, framed in the doorway, secure in her sturdy brogues and well-worn Fair Isle sweater, her long silver hair cascading almost to her waist.

Irene and Pam got out of the SUV and scurried up the walkway and onto the front porch, holding their jackets open over their heads to protect them from the rain.

"Don't you have an umbrella?" Neva asked.

Irene grinned sheepishly. "I do, but I left it in the back. It's now buried under boxes of aprons, placemats, and tablecloths."

Neva motioned them into the foyer and closed the door against the rain. The two women stood, water dripping off of their clothes and onto the rug.

Irene walked to the arched entrance to the small tea room off of the foyer. "You're packed in there. I should have known. Looks like they're all tourists, getting out of the rain."

"Yep. A downpour is always good for business. Were you coming in for tea?" She ran her eyes over them both and paused when she got to Pam's face.

"We were, but I can see you're full—and nobody in there looks like they're in a hurry to get going. We'll clear out of here…"

Neva put out her hand to block Irene's retreat while she kept her gaze on Pam. "No. You need to be here. You need to have some of Janie's specialty tea." She addressed Pam. "Tea with lavender honey, I think."

"That sounds fine," Pam said. "Why lavender?"

"Lavender heals broken hearts." Neva spoke quietly. "Come with me. I'm going to put you in my private sitting room. I just lit the fire when it started to rain. I take my tea in there every afternoon."

"We don't want to intrude…" Irene began as Neva moved off down a long hallway, beckoning them to follow her.

Neva opened a door at the end of the hall. "Settle yourselves. I'll go make the tea." She reached out a hand and briefly cupped Pam's cheek. "Try to empty your mind and take deep breaths. Everything is working out as it should, for your greater good." She turned and was gone, closing the door behind her.

Pam and Irene stared at each other.

"What was that about?" Pam asked. "Is Neva psychic or something?"

"I'm not sure about that, but I do know that she understands people and what they need." Irene sank into one of a pair of leather, wing-backed chairs flanking the fireplace and gestured for Pam to take the matching chair.

Pam sat. She glanced at her mother, who had placed her hands, palms up, on the arms of the chair and was breathing deeply. She followed suit, doing her best to clear her racing thoughts from her mind. Images of

Lance, with Connie pressing herself against him, kept popping up. She played a mental whack-a-mole game as she slapped the unwanted pictures out of her consciousness.

Smells of scones coming closer down the hallway soon pushed away any other thoughts. Neva opened the sitting-room door. She carried a tray bearing a teapot nestled in a quilted cozy that Irene had made for her the Christmas before last, three blue-flowered china teacups, and the plate of scones. In the center of the tray was a cut-glass dish of honey. She set the tray on a side table.

Neva brought the honey to Pam and then Irene. "Can you smell the lavender?"

Both women nodded.

Neva poured tea into each cup and added a generous dollop of lavender honey in the one she handed to Pam. She pulled a footstool up to the fire and sat, cradling her cup on her knees.

"Oh, good," Irene said. "You can join us. I was hoping you would."

Neva stretched out her legs to the fire and flexed her feet. "I've got everyone settled in the tea room, and Janie helps me on weekend afternoons. I can take a few minutes." She brought her feet back under herself and started to rise. "Would you like a scone? They're Carly's blueberry with vanilla glaze creations, and I have to say, she's mastered the recipe better than I ever could."

"I'm so glad you have the girls here now, Neva. I'm sure they're good company."

Neva nodded. "They really are. They've all made my life much easier, and also much happier. And my waistline bigger, too. Just wait until you taste these concoctions."

"Let me at 'em," Pam said, putting her cup on the hearth and leaping out of her seat. She placed a scone for each of them on a dessert plate and passed the plates around. "I'll gladly do some extra squats tomorrow to make up for it."

Neva took a sip of her tea. "Are you enjoying being back in Linden Falls?"

Pam nodded, her mouth full of scone.

"I hear you bought your grandmother's old place and are fixing it up. Doing most of the work yourself?"

"I am." Pam smiled. "I love doing it—and I'm learning a lot in the process. I just wish I had more time to work on it. At the rate I'm going, I'll never be done."

Neva nodded. "Some projects are meant to take a lifetime."

"Like running this inn," Pam said.

"Or raising a family," Irene said and instantly regretted it as a curtain of sadness dropped over Pam's face.

Neva looked between mother and daughter. "I remember when you got married and left Linden Falls." She addressed Pam. "I thought you were gone for good. You had tied your wish for a happy marriage and a family on the Wishing Tree and it had been granted," Neva said, referring to the giant linden tree in the square that everyone for miles around called the Wishing Tree.

Pam turned her face away. "That's not the way things worked out. I think that the"—she stopped herself before she said the word *stupid*—"Wishing Tree just isn't…" She paused again, searching for words that wouldn't hurt Neva's feelings. "Isn't for me."

Neva cocked her head to one side. "Do you still want a happy marriage and a family?"

Pam dropped her gaze to her lap.

"Just because the first guy wasn't 'the one' doesn't mean he's not out there—right now—waiting for you. Longing for you as much as you're longing for him."

Pam sighed heavily. "I…I just don't know. I'm not sure how I'd find him, anyway."

"What are you doing to look?" Neva asked.

Pam shrugged.

"I keep saying she should go on one of those online dating sites. Lots of people meet their soul mate that way. You hear about it all the time."

"Oh, Mom. I don't know anybody who's been happy with someone they've met online." Pam drained her teacup.

"I do," Neva said, looking at Pam over the rim of her teacup. "A second cousin's daughter in Florida found her husband that way. They're expecting their first child next month." She took Pam's empty cup to the tea tray and refilled it, adding an even more generous spoonful of honey than she'd put in the first one. Neva winked at Irene as Pam carefully accepted the full cup.

"I guess I could try it."

Irene practically bounced in her chair. "That's wonderful, honey. And I know just which photo you should use in your profile."

Pam lifted her eyebrows.

Irene dug her phone out of her purse and began scrolling through her photos. She tapped the screen when she found what she was looking for and chuckled as she held the phone out to Pam and Neva.

They both leaned close to see a snapshot of Pam, standing in the dappled sunshine underneath the Wishing Tree. Her chestnut hair curled below her shoulders, and her smile radiated happiness.

"That was the day I closed on the purchase of Grandma's house," Pam exclaimed.

"You were so happy—so proud of yourself," Irene said.

"That's it! That's the photo to use. Now all you have to do is fill out your profile and trust the process," Neva said.

Pam took another sip from her tea and looked between the two faces turned to her with such hope and expectation. "All right. Enough. If it will get the two of you to give me some peace for a while, I'll do it."

Neva and Irene beamed at each other.

"But don't get your hopes up. I'll give it thirty days. We'll see what happens," Pam said.

"You're making a start," Neva said. "That's what counts. Even God himself can't drive a parked car."

CHAPTER 4

*I*rene pulled her SUV alongside Pam's Prius in the dental office parking lot. The rain that had started in midafternoon continued, unabated, as the canopy of clouds forced an early twilight. Irene turned to her daughter. "Do you want to come over and have dinner with me?"

Thunder rumbled in the distance.

"I'm stuffed from all those scones. I won't need dinner tonight."

"Are you sure you'll be okay? You've had a nasty shock."

"I'll be fine. I need to get home and feed Leopold and spend some time with him." She brought her hand to her mouth to cover a yawn. "To be honest, I'm exhausted. I want to take a long bath and go through my Pinterest board on backsplash tile ideas. I'm almost ready to tackle that project."

Irene locked eyes with Pam. "You call me if you change your mind—or if you want to talk. Okay?"

"Of course." Pam leaned over and kissed her mother's cheek. She reached for her door handle and ready to spring out into the deluge when Irene stopped her.

"Why don't you set up your online dating profile instead of looking at those pins you've already examined dozens of times? I think you already know what tile you want to order." She raised her eyebrows and looked at Pam over the top of her glasses.

Pam leaned back against the seat. The windshield wipers slapped rhythmically. She took a deep breath, then released it slowly.

"You promised Neva and me."

"I guess I did. All right—I'll sign up with an online dating site, and I'll create my profile tonight."

"That's my girl," Irene said, patting Pam's arm. "I have such a good feeling about this."

Pam rolled her eyes. "I'm glad one of us does." She pulled her key fob from her purse and pushed the button to unlock her car. "Drive carefully getting home," she said as she opened the door and flung herself across the short distance to her car.

IRENE WAITED until Pam started the Prius and pulled out of her parking spot. Pam turned right, headed for the little house that had signaled her intention to make Linden Falls her home, while Irene took a left.

She had to admit—the idea of a long bath sounded irresistible. She'd unload the unsold inventory, tally up the day's receipts, and then fill her old, claw-footed tub with the bath salts she'd purchased from one of the other vendors at the market. The woman had told her the salts would ease her tired muscles and assure her a good night's sleep. It was time to put them to the test.

Irene drove along the square, deserted now in the inclement weather, with no trace remaining of the bustling farmers' market earlier in the day. She was almost abreast of the stately linden tree when the sun slashed through the clouds, illuminating it like an actor stepping into the spotlight on a stage. For decades, people had written their wishes, hopes, and dreams onto scraps of paper and tied them to its generous branches. The tree shielded and nurtured these wishes while their authors worked and waited for them to come true.

She angled the SUV into a spot at the curb and sat, drinking in the sight of the Wishing Tree. Pam might not believe in its properties, but Irene sure did. Hadn't she tied to the tree her wish that Pam would find her way back to Linden Falls—after Lance had broken her heart—only a week before her mother's former home was supposed to have gone on the market? Pam had made an offer on her grandmother's house and was now back for good. The Wishing Tree worked.

Irene was about to put the SUV into reverse and

resume her drive home when an idea hit her. She sat, deep in thought. She didn't know if it was acceptable to be so specific with a wish—especially when it involved two lives other than her own.

She finally shook her head as if dislodging any doubts and got out of the SUV. She walked to the famous tree with its immense canopy of branches. A wooden box beneath the tree contained pieces of paper and small lengths of ribbon. She scribbled her wish on one of the papers and read it over, underlining the two names on the paper—twice—with bold slashes. They were perfect for each other. She was positive.

Irene closed her eyes and spun around until she felt moved to stop. She opened her eyes and secured her wish to the first branch she saw.

Irene stepped back. Her wish was tied at a spot where two branches joined into one. Chills ran down her spine. A good omen, she thought. Irene touched her fingertips to her lips, then pressed them to the tree where her wish was now tied. She turned and walked back to her SUV, a sense of happiness in her heart and a lightness in her step that she hadn't felt in years.

NEVA WAS PULLING the curtains closed on the window in her office when she noticed Irene hurrying away from the Wishing Tree. She smiled to herself. Her friend must have been tying a wish to the tree. She had a pretty good idea what Irene had wished for.

WORKOUT WISHES & VALENTINE KISSES

Neva gathered up the soggy papers she'd retrieved from the tree right before the afternoon's storm had hit. As the official wish keeper, she had taken it upon herself to save the wishes from destruction by the elements. She took them down and stored them in plastic sleeves inserted into binders, each meticulously marked with dates and times.

She'd spread out today's haul on the long service table in the now-empty tea room. They would dry by the fire, and she'd put them into their plastic sleeves and tuck them away in a binder before she went to bed. But first, she needed to run across the street to the Wishing Tree and gather up Irene's wish. The momentary burst of sunshine was long gone, and rain-drops were beginning to patter against her windowpane.

Neva shoved her arms into the jacket she kept hanging by the front door—the one with a pair of scis-sors in the right pocket—and pulled her long hair out of the collar. She tied a scarf around her head and headed out into the light rain.

Her rubber-soled brogues provided sure footing, and she made her way to the tree and back in no time. She walked to the table and placed Irene's wish on the end, nodding as she read it. She had been correct about what she'd thought Irene had wished for.

Neva was untying her scarf when her eye fell on the wish that lay diagonally to the left of Irene's. She read this other wish, then reread Irene's wish. A smile that seemed to start at her toes and end at the top of her head spread over her lips. She knew what she had to do.

She picked up both wishes and cleared a space for them in the center of the table. She'd seen simultaneous wishes before and knew what this meant. For now, her part would be to keep the wishes together in the binder until they came together in real life.

CHAPTER 5

Steve Turner opened the door marked "Personal Trainers Only." The small room was reserved as a private space for the personal trainers who worked at Linden Falls Fitness. A row of lockers ran along the wall to the left of the door. A rectangular folding table on the far wall corralled a microwave, a coffee machine, and a basket containing sweeteners, stir sticks, and extra packets of red pepper flakes, Parmesan cheese, and soy sauce—all left over from takeout food hastily consumed at the table.

Two folding chairs were pulled up to the table. A mirror hung on the wall opposite the lockers. Underneath the mirror was a leather sofa that one of the trainers had found at an estate sale. The trainers had all chipped in to defray its cost. Slumped against one of the sofa's oversized arms was Pam Olson, her eyes half-closed.

"Hey," Steve said. "You look exhausted." At six foot

four and two hundred forty-five pounds, the former professional football player's athletic form dominated the small room. He pointed to the cup of coffee she clutched in her hand. "I've never seen you drink coffee in the middle of the day. Tough weekend?" He flashed his bigger-than-life smile at his coworker and friend.

"It was okay." She stifled a yawn and took a sip of her coffee.

"Just okay? Did something go wrong with whatever home improvement project you're working on? You know you can always call me if you get into a bind and need help. My ex and I—correction, *I*—did a lot of remodeling of our house when we were married."

"You're such a nice guy, you know that?" Pam shook her head. "I didn't work on my house this weekend. I helped my mom at the market on Saturday and spent Sunday on the computer."

"Driving yourself nuts, looking at…what are they called? Pins? on DIY projects?" He made himself a cup of coffee and sat at the other end of the sofa.

"No. I got the fliers ready for the Christmas toy drive." She rose and opened her locker, removing one of the fliers. "What do you think?"

"Nice! Very eye-catching. They look professional."

She snorted as he handed the paper back to her.

"No, really, you could have been a graphic designer."

A smile played at the corners of her lips. "They did turn out pretty well."

"I'm so glad you're here to work on the drive with me this year. It's one of my favorite things to do during the holidays, but it's a lot of work for one person. Like those fliers—mine were never that good. When do you want to put them up around town?"

"The Fall Festival on the square is this weekend. There's already tons of stuff posted around town promoting it. I thought we should wait until next week when all of that's come down."

"I agree. How about Tuesday after lunch, during the early afternoon lull." He pulled out his phone and consulted his calendar. "I've got a break from noon until three."

"Me, too," she said, sinking back into her seat on the sofa. "We can take them to the shopkeepers around the square. Then we can hit town hall, the post office, the library, Aspen Grove senior center— all the usual, high-traffic places. I know Paige at Town Square Books would also let us post some there."

"Excellent." He cocked his head to one side, and his deep espresso eyes searched her face. "Something's got your goat. What happened this weekend?"

"I…I ran into Lance."

"What?" Steve erupted.

"And his new girlfriend. Our old next-door neighbor." She swallowed hard and tried to hide the pain she still felt.

"Ouch! That must have hurt. Was this the first time you've seen him?"

She nodded, losing her grip on the misery she'd been keeping bottled up since Friday night.

"That's rough. The first time is the worst. Where did you run into him—them?"

The whole sad story tumbled out of Pam.

"That bastard! He did that on purpose to hurt you." He leaned forward and ground his fist into his palm. "I'd like to kick his ass."

Pam smiled and patted his forearm. "You're still like a protective big brother to me, aren't you?"

"Always! I hate seeing my best friend's kid sister get treated this way." He looked into her eyes, and his expression was serious. "He was never good enough for you—not by a long shot. You're better off without him."

"Thank you. That's what Mom says. She and Neva talked me into registering with an online dating service. That's what I spent most of my time doing on Sunday—setting up my profile."

"I don't know about those dating sites." Steve was shaking his head. "Just be careful, okay? There are lots of creeps out there. And very needy people."

Pam raised an eyebrow. "Have you tried them?"

"A long time ago. I logged at least two lifetimes of terrible dates in just a few months."

"Really? What was so bad about them?"

"I seemed to attract women who were looking for someone to save them. You couldn't tell that from their profiles, of course, but it always came out after a while. I don't need someone to save me, and I'm not interested in rescuing someone else. I wanted an independent woman who had her act together."

"That doesn't sound like too much to ask for. I'm hoping to find a self-reliant man, too."

"I wish you better luck than I had. I finally got off the sites. In fact, I'm taking a total break from dating, and I've never been happier."

Pam considered his words. For someone touting how happy he was, he certainly didn't look happy.

"As I said, just be careful. Make sure someone knows who you're meeting and where. You can—"

Pam held up her hand to stop him. "I've read all the rules and guidelines. You don't need to worry about me."

"Good. I'd hate to lose the second-best trainer in this gym."

Pam guffawed as he got to his feet. He crumpled his paper coffee cup and sent it sailing into the trash. "I've got a client in two minutes."

"I do, too," Pam said.

Steve pulled her to her feet.

"Let's get out there and give these folks their money's worth."

Pam smiled at him. "Thanks for making me feel better. You always do."

CHAPTER 6

*P*am nodded at the older woman as she entered the weight room for her training session. Barb McVey was a cheerful woman in her sixties whose energy level and industry amazed Pam. Trim and flexible, Barb had never missed a session with Pam in the year that they'd been working together.

"Let's start on your chest," Pam said, pointing to a bench.

Barb lay down and extended her hands to receive the twelve-pound weights Pam handed her.

"How was your weekend?" Pam asked.

"Very productive," Barb said, huffing with exertion as she pushed the weights up and down. "I wrote another six thousand words in the novel I'm working on."

"You're incredible. Most people your age are content to putter around with their hobbies and watch TV."

"Not me. That'd drive me nuts." Barb stood, and they began to exercise her biceps. "I've got a publishing deadline looming over my head. I'll get it done—I always do. Did you work on more of your DIY projects for your house?"

Pam shook her head. "Let's do another set of chest presses."

Barb resumed her position on the bench. "I forgot—you help your mother with her booth at the farmers' market during the fall."

"That was Saturday." Pam took a deep breath, then plunged ahead. "I spent Sunday setting up my online profile for a dating service."

Barb finished her final set of presses and practically jumped off the bench. "Really? Oh, I'm so thrilled to hear this."

Pam glanced at Barb, who was beaming at her.

"What made you finally get started?"

Barb's delight made Pam smile. "I guess I finally couldn't resist you and my mom and Neva. You all insisted I give it a try—so I did."

Barb clasped her hands in front of her. "Well...what do you think?"

"It's been pretty interesting, actually. It's fun to see what other people post about themselves. I'm just getting started on the site. There are a lot of people out there looking for someone."

"Has anyone caught your eye?"

"There is one guy..." Pam walked Barb to the leg

sled machine.

Barb climbed into the sled and began to do her reps. "Okay—spill the beans on him."

"He's a divorced father of two. Says he's thirty-eight. He's an electrical engineer and works for the power company."

"Educated, smart—and employed. All good things," Barb said.

"That's what I thought. We both like to read, and he's remodeled his house, so we have that in common."

"Have you met?"

"Not yet. We've talked on the phone."

"How's that been?"

"He's a little"—Pam paused, then shrugged—"boring, to be honest."

Barb clicked her tongue. "It's way too early to make judgments," she insisted. "Some people just aren't phone people. I think you need to meet him before you decide one way or the other."

"That's what my mom said."

Barb nodded her agreement. "See—listen to us older and wiser women."

"I guess it wouldn't hurt to have coffee with him."

Barb snapped her fingers. "I've got an even better idea. Why don't you go to the Fall Festival together? It's supposed to be a lovely weekend, and you won't be stuck at a table, trying to make conversation. Instead, you'll be walking around, seeing all kinds of things that will give you lots to talk about. There's food and activities. And you'll be in the midst of the entire town, so you'll be completely safe. It's the perfect first date."

"That's not a bad idea," Pam said.

"Even if he's a dud—which I'm sure he won't be—you can still enjoy yourself."

"We're supposed to talk tonight. I'll suggest it."

"Good for you!" Barb pumped a fist in the air. "And even if he doesn't work out, you've made a start. That's the important thing. There'll always be another one."

"I appreciate your enthusiasm," Pam said, "but I'm not so sure about that."

"You're a wonderful woman, Pam," Barb said, "and I think you'd make a terrific partner. Take it from me; a happy marriage is worth waiting for. There's a man out there who is longing to find you. All you have to do is be open to the possibility."

Pam felt her face begin to flush. "From your lips to God's ears," she said. "And now, we've got to step up the pace if we're going to finish your workout before my next client."

"Got it," Barb said, stepping into a lunge.

CHAPTER 7

*P*am released the breath she'd been holding when she spotted Chris Harris at the edge of the crowd. Taller than she'd expected, he towered over the people milling around the balloon arch that marked the entrance to the forty-eighth annual Fall Festival. She raised her hand and waved it over her head to get his attention.

The moon was almost full and, together with illumination supplied by overhead rented lights, visibility at the festival was good. Chris finally spotted her and made his way toward her, drawing up short when two young boys darted in front of him, heedless of his presence. He stumbled, then regained his footing.

Pam watched Chris turn in the boys' direction and call something to them that she couldn't hear. He frowned as he approached and his eyes were hashtags of wrinkles. The skin on his neck sagged. Even from five feet away, Pam could tell that he had to be at least ten years older than he'd stated in his online profile.

She drew a deep breath and forced her lips into a smile. It was too late to run away. Besides, she needed to give this guy a chance. Pam extended her hand. "You must be Chris."

He grasped her fingertips and squeezed them awkwardly in a gesture that was more aligned with kissing her hand than a handshake. "Yes. Sorry I'm late. The parking for this event was a nightmare. I was circling the square, looking for a spot, for at least twenty minutes. The signage for offsite parking was confusing and inadequate—"

Pam interrupted him. "You're here now. That's all that matters."

"I hate to be late. And I hate being inconvenienced by incompetence."

"Fortunately, we're not trying to make a curtain call. We've got more than enough time to enjoy the festival. Shall we take a walk around to see what's here and decide what we want to see more of?" She reached into a paper bag that she held by its handles, withdrawing a paper sleeve of kettle corn and passing it to him. "This is my favorite thing at the fair. I've been eating it my whole life. I came early just to snag us some, so we didn't have to spend all evening waiting in line." She pointed across the square to where a long string of people snaked along the perimeter. "They'll be there at least half an hour." She retrieved her sleeve of the treat and began to munch.

Chris handed his back to her. "This stuff is full of sugar and trans-fat. I'd never eat this."

She raised her eyes to his as she brought another mouthful to her lips.

"But you enjoy yours," he stammered. "I'm sure once a year won't hurt you."

She opened her mouth and inserted the popcorn.

"I'm just saying that I would never do it."

Pam put both sleeves of kettle corn back into the carrier bag. She'd enjoy her treat later, when she wasn't under his censoring eye.

They began to walk. "What are your fondest childhood memories from the fall?" she asked.

"I used to love carving my pumpkin. I was an only child, as you may have seen from my bio. Our family would go to a local farm to let me pick out my pumpkin. I'd bring it home and spend hours figuring out how I wanted to carve it."

"That sounds fun," Pam said. "Did you go for the biggest pumpkin?"

"Not necessarily. I was more interested in the shape and symmetry of the pumpkin. I really got into it."

"Scary or friendly?"

"Scary." He smiled at her, and he had a nice smile.

"They have a pumpkin-carving contest here at the festival. There are divisions for kids, based on age brackets, and an adult section. Let's go check it out." Pam led him to the long rows of tables containing pumpkins. They wove their way through the tables, examining the entrants. A placard at each one gave the carver's name and age.

"Some of these children are truly talented," Pam said, bending over to examine the intricate carving created by a girl of eleven. "I'm afraid I never graduated beyond triangles for eyes and a toothy smile." She glanced over her shoulder at him. "Would you have entered one of these contests when you were a kid?"

Chris shrugged. "Possibly."

She waited for him to continue, but he remained silent. "What do you think about the adult entries?"

"They're passable," he said. "I think I could do better."

Pam's shoulders tensed. "Maybe you can carve one next year for the competition. It'd be fun to win."

"I wouldn't have the time."

"I'm sure it doesn't take all that long to carve a pumpkin," she said, trying to keep her rising irritation out of her voice.

He had already moved on and didn't hear her.

They walked toward the bandstand where "Hocus Pocus" played on a continuous loop. A booming voice called her name.

Pam knew that voice and quickened her pace. The last thing she wanted to do was introduce her "date" to Steve.

Steve called to her again.

She wouldn't be able to ignore him. Pam touched Chris's arm to get his attention and turned to see Steve sprinting over to them.

"Hi!" Steve extended his hand to Chris. "I'm Steve Turner. I work with Pam at Linden Falls Fitness."

"Ah…I'm Chris Harris."

Steve shifted his gaze to Pam. "So…are you enjoying the festival?"

"We are," Pam said with a cheeriness she didn't feel. "What are you doing here? I didn't expect to see you."

"I'm with my sister and her family. My niece and nephews begged me to come. Emma entered a pumpkin in the competition. She's eight." He lowered his voice and stepped closer. "Between you and me, I don't think she has a chance of winning, but she's really excited about hearing them announce the winners at eight thirty."

"That's sweet of you to be here for them," Pam said.

"I'm having a blast, to be honest with you. I'm usually so tired on Friday nights that I go home after work and veg out in front of the TV. This is so much better."

A boy who looked to be about ten raced up to them and tugged on Steve's sleeve. "It's almost our turn to go into the maze," he said breathlessly. "Come on, Uncle Steve."

"I'd better go. Have you done the maze? It's made up of bales of hay. It's supposed to be pretty neat. Why don't you join us?"

"That'd be nice—" Pam began before Chris cut her off.

"I'm allergic to hay," Chris said, "and I left my inhaler at home. I can't go near that thing."

"Go on—and enjoy yourselves," Pam said to Steve as his nephew pulled him toward the maze.

Pam and Chris took one more lap around the festival before Chris began to rub his hands along his arms. "I should have worn a warmer jacket," he said.

"It is getting a bit chilly," Pam agreed.

"I think I'd better be going," he said. "I don't want to catch cold."

"Of course not," Pam said, a growing sense of relief washing over her.

"I'll walk you to your car," Chris said. "I'm parked over here." He pointed behind him.

"That's not necessary," Pam said. "I'm in the opposite direction—right along the square. I'll be perfectly safe getting to my car. No sense in you staying out here in the cold any longer than necessary."

"You're sure?"

"Absolutely."

"Okay. Thank you for a nice evening."

"I'm glad you enjoyed yourself." Pam fumbled on the words, certain he had done no such thing.

Chris leaned toward her.

A large retriever bounded between them, dragging her leash, with Paige from the bookstore in hot pursuit. "Excuse me," she said as the dog ran between them.

"Oh, hi, Paige," Pam called out, but Paige and her dog, Gladys, were gone too fast.

"That was rude," Chris said, watching them run off.

"No, not really. Usually Gladys is free to roam town without a leash, but with so many people here for the festival, Paige must've wanted to keep her closer. She's a sweet dog, and believe me, Paige isn't a rude person."

He gave a disapproving snort.

Pam stepped back. "Drive safely getting home," she said, moving even farther away.

Chris nodded and turned to walk to his car.

Pam inhaled deeply. Her shoulders untensed for the first time that evening, and the night air revived her spirits. She checked her watch—it was only eight. She toyed with the idea of waiting for the pumpkin-carving contest winners to be announced in thirty minutes, then decided against it. Instead, she withdrew her unfinished sleeve of kettle corn from her carrier bag and shoved a large handful in her mouth. She'd finish both sleeves—now suddenly glad that Chris hadn't wanted his—and make it an early night. It might have been a disastrous date, but she had two bags of kettle corn to look forward to.

CHAPTER 8

*S*teve handed Brian McVey a set of weights, and his client immediately got to business. After training together for almost ten years, they both knew the drill.

"Were the fish biting this weekend?" Brian asked.

"They were okay," Steve said. "It's starting to be too cold. Next weekend might be my last time to go."

"I've never understood the attraction of fishing," Brian said. "It's too quiet for me."

"That's what I like about it. Frankly, I don't care if I catch anything or not."

"Don't you get bored?"

"Nope. I like being out in nature. I can slow down and let my mind drift. It's sort of meditative."

"I can see that. I feel the same way on the golf course."

Steve loaded a bar with weights, and they moved to chest presses.

"Barb thought she saw you at the festival Saturday night—with a woman with three kids."

"Yep. That's my sister and her brood. Her husband is an emergency room physician and had to work, so I came along to help corral the kids."

"She said it looked like you were having a lot of fun —that you're a natural with kids."

Steve took the bar from Brian, and they moved to a machine to do squats. "Where's this conversation going, Brian?"

"You know Barb—she thinks the world of you. She wants you to be happy."

"I am happy."

"You know what I mean—happily married."

"Not everybody is as lucky as you and Barb."

"That may be true, but we both think you're one of those people who would make a great partner. And dad. Having children is the greatest pleasure in life."

Steve shook his head. "I admit, I'd like to have had kids. But been there, done that on the whole marriage thing. And dating just filled my life with drama—and expense."

"Oh, come on. It can't have been that bad."

"Trust me—it was. I'm better off on my own."

"Now—"

"Do I have to pile on so much weight that you can't keep talking?"

Brian held up a hand. "Don't do that. I'll butt out of your business. For now."

They were almost finished with their session when

Brian pointed over Steve's shoulder toward the doorway to the weight room.

Pam stood, a thick stack of papers clutched against her chest, looking in their direction. Steve nodded at her.

"Now that's the sort of girl you should be interested in," Brian said. "She trains my wife. Barb says she's nice and smart. And she's interested in fitness, just like you are. Plus, she's a real looker. Why don't you ask her out?"

"I've known Pam since we were kids. Her older brother was my best bud. She's all of those things, for sure. We're great friends, and I don't want to jeopardize that. I also don't want to risk any personal drama here at the gym."

"Suit yourself, but remember: nothing ventured, nothing gained." Brian grabbed his water bottle from where it sat at his feet. "See you next time. I've got to get out of here. I'm meeting Barb at the Crooked Porch Café for lunch, and I think someone needs a word with you." He gestured with his head to Pam.

"Have a good lunch," Steve said. He walked over to Pam.

"Is this still a good time to distribute these?" she asked, raising the stack of fliers in her hand.

"Yep. I don't have another client until three. How about you?"

"I'm free until then, too. We should be able to get these posted before we need to be back here."

"We'll take care of the merchants along the square

for sure." They headed for the parking lot. "I've got the cardboard boxes for toy collection in the back of my truck. They're easy to set up. Why don't you ride with me?" He led the way to his truck and opened her door for her.

"You don't need to do that," she said, gesturing to the door.

"My mother would tan my hide if she heard I hadn't opened a car door for a lady."

Pam laughed. "You're an old-school gentleman. Tell your mother I think she did a great job with you."

Steve felt himself flush. He got into the truck and started it up. "So…how was your date Saturday night? With…what was his name?"

"Chris." Pam inhaled slowly and turned to look out the passenger window. "Okay, I guess."

"That doesn't sound like a rousing endorsement."

"I'm sure he's a nice enough man. I mean, he didn't do anything wrong. Not really."

Steve glanced over at her and remained silent.

"It's just that he wasn't any fun. He was critical of everything. I found myself looking at my watch every five minutes, wishing the evening were over."

"I know that feeling," Steve said.

"He left before the winners of the pumpkin-carving contests were announced. I was so worn out from being with him that I went straight home and crashed. In the past, when I've been on my own at the fall festival, I've stayed until they turn the lights out."

Steve angled into a parking spot along the square. "You felt more alone than if you'd been by yourself?"

"I did."

"That sort of loneliness—the kind you feel when you're with someone you don't belong with—is the absolute worst. Believe me; I've experienced that feeling dozens—no, hundreds—of times. No, thank you."

"Is that why you don't date?"

"Exactly. My life has been so much better now that I've decided to give up on the whole thing."

They got out of the car. Pam clutched the fliers while Steve took a stack of flattened cardboard boxes out of the back of his truck.

"I have to admit," Pam said, as they headed toward Town Square Books, "I felt depressed all day Sunday after that disappointing date. I'm not sure I want to go through months—maybe even years—of this process while I'm trying to find 'the one.' I'm not even sure I believe there's someone out there for me."

"I understand," he replied. "Each time things didn't work out, I felt worse than before. I finally asked myself why I kept beating my head against the wall. Take it from me; it's not worth it."

"It's just that my mom—and Neva and Barb—keep pushing me."

"Neva was on my case about getting remarried for the longest time, too. I finally told her I'd taken a no-dating pledge, and she backed off." He swung to face her. "Why don't you join me in the pledge? When

49

anyone asks, you can tell them that you've got to honor your pledge."

Pam laughed. "You think that'll stop them?"

They reached the door into the bookstore, and Steve stopped walking. "Honestly? I think it'll help you stick to your guns. Like when workout buddies promise each other they're going to meet at the gym. They keep going because they're accountable to someone else. I think that'll work the same way for us."

"You're serious, aren't you?"

Steve nodded.

Pam cocked her head to one side. "You may be right. I'll think about it."

"You should."

"I'm just getting started on this dating website. I should give it some time."

"Sounds like somebody needs to go on more disastrous dates before she makes up her mind."

"That's an optimistic viewpoint!"

"I'm just telling it like it is." Steve looked at Pam. "I hope I'm wrong. You're a terrific gal—you deserve to be happy."

Pam blushed and turned away from him.

"The offer still stands. You can join me in the pledge anytime."

CHAPTER 9

*P*am and Steve stepped inside the Crooked Porch Café. Steve raised his hand to signal the hostess at the back of the restaurant.

She began walking toward them, smiling broadly when she got close enough to see what Steve was holding. "I've cleared a spot for the toy drive donation box right over there." She pointed to the floor in front of a bay window. "Our Christmas tree always goes there. We'll put the collection box next to it."

"That'll be perfect," Pam said. "When people pass by on the sidewalk, they'll be able to see all the toys piling up."

"It'll make people want to come in to donate," the hostess said.

Steve unfolded the flaps on one of the cardboard collection boxes and set it in place while Pam taped one of her fliers to the front window.

"Stand there, like you're a Christmas tree," Pam said

to Steve. "I'll go outside to see what it'll look like from the sidewalk."

Steve turned toward the window and raised his hands over his head, touching his fingertips together to form a triangle.

Pam sauntered by slowly, turning her head to look in the window. Steve stuck out his tongue, and Pam threw her head back and laughed. She reentered the restaurant. "Nice impersonation of a Christmas tree," she chided Steve.

"How'd it look in here?" he asked.

"Let's scoot our collection box a foot to the right," Pam said. "It'll be more visible from the outside."

Steve made the suggested adjustment.

Pam was gathering the remainder of her fliers from the hostess stand when she heard her name being called. She spun around and searched for the familiar voice.

Barb McVey pushed back her chair and was halfway out of her seat when Pam spotted her. Brian stood and gestured for Pam and Steve to come to their table.

"What a lovely surprise," Barb said when they were within earshot. "It's so nice to see the two of you out together, away from the gym."

"We're not really 'out together,'" Pam replied quickly.

"We're distributing fliers and collection boxes for the annual toy drive," Steve said.

Barb and Brian were seated next to each other at a

table for four. Brian pulled back one of the empty chairs. "Why don't you join us for lunch?"

"Thank you—that's a very nice offer," Pam replied. "But we've still got to distribute all of these"—she tapped the stack of papers in her arms—"and be back in time for our three o'clock clients."

"The service here is speedy," Brian said. "You've got to eat."

Pam and Steve exchanged a glance before Steve spoke. "We're on a mission—and we're already behind."

"If you say so." Barb shrugged, unable to conceal her disappointment.

"Good to see you," Steve said. "And thank you, again, for the invitation. We'd better be on our way."

"Enjoy your lunch," Pam said as they turned and beat a hasty retreat out of the restaurant.

Barb and Brian watched them go.

"You're right," Barb said to her husband. "They'd be perfect together. I don't know why I didn't see it before."

"Like I told you, I was just saying that to Steve before I left the gym to pick you up. When you called her name, and I saw them together, I thought maybe he'd taken my advice to heart."

Barb reached over and squeezed her husband's arm. "That's one of the many things I love about you— you're a romantic through and through. You believe in a happy ending for everyone."

Brian put his hand on top of hers. "After I met you, I

learned how fulfilling life could be when you share it with the right person."

Barb's eyes glistened. "You are the most marvelous man." She blinked rapidly. "And you want what we have for both of them."

"I do."

"Me, too. We just have to figure out how to get them together."

"What's her story?"

"Messy divorce, soured on men. Irene and Neva recently convinced her to set up a profile on an online dating app."

"At least she's open to a new relationship. Steve won't even entertain the idea of dating."

"That's a shame. They have such an easy cama-raderie. And chemistry—I can feel it."

Brian pursed his lips. "I don't know how to change his mind."

Barb snapped her fingers. "I have an idea. At least it's a place to start." She rummaged in her purse and pulled out a pen. She reached for a paper napkin.

Brian leaned over her shoulder and stared at the napkin as she wrote.

"Do you have string?" Barb asked.

Brian shook his head. "You're not going to hang that on the Wishing Tree, are you? You can't believe in all that nostalgic folklore."

"*We* most certainly are going to hang it, and I *do* believe in it." Barb fixed Brian with her gaze.

He threw up his hands. "There's paper and ribbon in a wooden box at the tree."

"That's right. I forgot," Barb said. "I'll rewrite this on one of those papers. Let's finish our sandwiches and get this wish into place. Something tells me we've got no time to lose."

CHAPTER 10

*P*am walked to the front of the classroom and smiled at the woman setting up her weights on a mat in front of three rows of women ready for class. Susan Wilbanks reminded her of a peacock in her skintight spandex accented with stripes and swooshes of neon mesh fabric. The others were attired in yoga pants and oversized T-shirts. To be fair, Susan's body was sculpted to perfection, and she looked like she'd stepped right out of an advertisement for the active wear molded to her body.

"Hi," Pam said. "You must have heard that Joan's daughter sprained her ankle at school this morning, and she had leave to take her to the emergency room."

Susan straightened a pair of fifteen-pound dumb-bells on her mat and stood to face Pam. "Yes. I over-heard her tell the person at the front desk as she was leaving the building. I've attended this power pump class for years. I figured I could lead the class today."

She slid her eyes to the group of retired women who were now staring at them. "It's not like any of them are doing anything difficult."

Pam's eyes narrowed. "Everyone's doing the best they can." She bent over and picked up the dumbbells. "I'll be filling in for Joan today, so I'll help you move your stuff—there's an open spot in the back."

"I'm capable of leading this class."

"Unless you've been trained and certified as an instructor, the gym can't allow it. Insurance and all that." She glanced at Susan, whose facial coloring now bordered on the neon red in her outfit. "Look, I appreciate that you're willing to help. That's nice of you."

Susan shrugged and picked up her barbell. "Suit yourself. I can move my own stuff," she said stiffly. "You'd better get your equipment. You're already starting class five minutes late as it is."

Pam turned to the class and was pleasantly surprised to see Barb in the middle row. At least there was one friendly face in the room. "I'm sorry that we're getting a late start. I'm going to talk you through a warm-up while I get myself set up. Pick up your light bar, and let's begin…"

For the next forty minutes, Pam led the class through a power pump routine that she'd taught at a gym in Boston—when she'd been married to Lance and had thought she'd been building a life with him.

Pam forced the memories from her mind. She dimmed the lights at the end of class and guided the group through her signature cooldown routine. Part stretching, part deep breathing, and part meditation, it had been her favorite part of teaching fitness classes.

As the participants were stowing their equipment in the weight room, one woman after another approached to thank her for stepping in.

"The cooldown was just wonderful," a woman said. "I'm relaxed and refreshed."

"I loved the change in our routine," another woman said. "Joan always does the exact same thing every time."

"There's nothing wrong with consistency," Susan interjected. "I think Joan is great."

"I do, too," Pam said.

Susan turned on her heel and stalked off.

"Ignore her. She gets her back up over the silliest things." Barb was standing behind her.

Pam turned to face Barb. "Thanks. I didn't know you took Joan's class."

"I have—for years. I started weight training with you because I had plateaued with her." She cocked her head to one side. "Is that okay? I never thought to ask if I could do both."

"It's fine. Helpful, actually."

Barb bit her lip. "Can I ask a favor?"

"Sure."

"I'm speaking for the whole class on this—except maybe Susan. Could you talk to Joan—encourage her to change things up a bit?"

"I can try," Pam said as they left the room and

walked down the hallway. "You know Joan better than I do. I'm not so sure she's open to suggestions."

"Just give it your best shot. We won't hold you to any results."

"You've got it," Pam said.

They turned the corner and almost ran into Steve.

"I was looking for you," he said to Pam. "The front desk told me you'd subbed for Joan."

"Did you check on the toy boxes? How're donations coming along?"

"Well…" He sucked in a breath. "Dismal, actually. We've got a couple of toys in the boxes at Duncan's Hardware and the Crooked Porch Café, plus one book in the box at Town Square Books, but that's it."

"Oh, no! That's awful."

"It's way less than we've gotten in the first week of collection in other years," Steve said, "but we're starting earlier this year than ever before."

"Should we have waited a week?" Pam asked.

"Maybe." Steve shrugged his shoulders.

"Now listen," Barb said. "The Linden Falls Toy Drive has always been a tremendous success, and it will be again this year. It's still two weeks until Thanksgiving, and the warm spell hasn't felt the least bit Christmassy."

"That's true," Pam said. "Do you think that could be it?"

"I'd bet on it. Just wait and see," Barb said. She looked between the two of them. "I think good things happen when the two of you team up on something."

Steve opened his mouth to reply, then shut it quickly. His eyes widened as he looked over Pam and Barb's shoulders. "I've got to go," he sputtered as he spun on his heel and jogged away.

"What in the world got into him?" Pam looked over her shoulder to see Susan approaching them like a lion stalking its prey.

"Where's Steve going?" Susan asked when she caught up to them. "I need to talk to him. Every time I see him, he's rushing off in the opposite direction."

"I've got no idea," Pam said truthfully.

"He's sure a tall drink of water," Barb said. "Too bad we're both happily married women, isn't it?" She looked pointedly at Susan.

Susan brushed her hair behind her shoulders and smoothed a nonexistent wrinkle from her spandex pants. "I've got to go," she said and walked away.

"If I were a betting person, I'd say she's after our Steve," Barb said.

"I think you're right," Pam agreed.

"Poor Steve," both women said in unison.

LATER THAT NIGHT, Barb and Brian settled onto the sofa to watch their favorite British crime drama on television. Barb patted the couch next to her, and their dachshund mix of uncertain pedigree sprang into his place on her lap. She began to massage the dog's silky ears.

Brian grabbed the remote.

"What've you got planned for tomorrow?" she asked him as the opening credits began to roll.

"I was going to start cleaning out the garage," he said. "The weather's been so nice, I thought I should take advantage of it. Before long, it'll be miserably cold out there."

"Oh…"

"Why? What would you like to do?"

"Something I heard at the gym today has been rolling around in my mind."

Brian pushed the pause button. "I'm intrigued. What's up?"

"I understand that donations to the toy drive are lagging."

"Really? It's early days. People just need to see that others are donating. You know—get them in the spirit."

Barb shifted her weight so she was facing him. "Exactly! I think we should do something about that."

"Like what?"

"Like give the donations a solid head start."

"You mean, prime the pump?"

"Yes! We could buy up a whole bunch of toys and distribute them around town."

"We'll fill up the back of the SUV. I love buying toys."

"That's the inner child in you." She took his hand in hers and squeezed it.

"We'll start first thing in the morning," he said. "Let's be at the store when they open at eight and buy as many toys as the SUV will hold. Our first stop can be the Crooked Porch Café. We'll put toys in their box —maybe cover the bottom of their box—then have breakfast there. We'll make a day of it."

"What about cleaning the garage? This mild weather won't last."

He laughed. "Cleaning the garage can wait. I'm pretty sure it'll still be a mess in a couple of days. Kicking this toy drive into gear is way more important."

Barb leaned over and kissed him. "You are the best husband ever."

"I'm excited for tomorrow," he replied, his eyes shining. "This is going to be fun."

CHAPTER 11

"*How* 'bout we head to Neva's for tea," Irene said as she and Pam packed up her booth at the farmers' market. "It was so much fun last week, and we were even busier today. We can make it our tradition."

"Tea was wonderful," Pam agreed, "but I need to get home to shower and do my makeup."

Irene's head snapped up. "You're going out—on a date?"

Pam nodded.

Irene clasped her hands together. "I'm delighted to hear this. I was afraid that you'd let that"—she paused, searching for the right words—"disappointing date at the Fall Festival put you off dating altogether."

"I was pretty discouraged, but I promised you and Neva that I'd give this online dating thing a thirty-day trial. I can't admit defeat after one try."

"That's my girl!" Irene beamed. "Will you call me in the morning to tell me how it goes?"

"You bet," Pam said.

Irene looked at her watch. "I can finish packing up. You've helped enough for one day. Go home and get ready." She snatched a stack of aprons from Pam's hands.

Pam leaned in and kissed her mother on the cheek. "If you're sure?"

"I'm positive. Have fun."

Pam began to move away.

"And don't forget to call me!"

>>))

"YES, MA'AM," the hostess said, smiling at Pam. "He's already been seated." She grabbed a leather-bound menu from the stack on the hostess stand. "Right this way."

The hostess led her to a table in the back corner of the restaurant. A blond man in a well-cut blue suit rose from his chair as he watched them approach.

Pam extended her hand across the table, and they introduced themselves. Mathew Dalton looked to be the age he had listed in his profile. Trim, tanned, and fit, his profile photo was a good likeness. She smiled at him with a sense of relief. The evening was off to a fine start.

"I'm sorry if you've been waiting for me," Pam said, checking her watch as he held her chair out for her. "I understood we weren't meeting until six. I thought I'd be here early."

"You are early," Mathew said. "We said six. I wanted to make sure we got a table where I could sit with my back to the wall."

Pam looked at him quizzically.

"Just a habit of mine," he said. "Have you eaten here before?"

"No. This place just opened. I've heard nothing but good things about the food."

The waiter interrupted their conversation to take their drink orders and recite the daily special.

Mathew turned to Pam. "That sea bass special with risotto sounds great. Why don't you pick out an appetizer?"

"Let's share one. What do you like?" Pam asked.

"Lady's choice. Surprise me."

Pam addressed the waiter. "Between the house-smoked salmon and the burrata and tomato on toast, which do you suggest?"

"If one of you is having the sea bass, you might want to start with the burrata," he said.

"Good point," Pam said. "I'd like the sea bass special, too. Do you like burrata?" Pam asked Mathew.

"Honestly, I've never had it. Tonight is a time to try new things. Let's have the burrata," Mathew told the waiter. "And two of the sea bass specials."

"Excellent choices," the waiter said, scribbling on his order pad and moving away.

"How did you spend your day?" Mathew asked, giving her his full attention.

Pam described the busy morning at the farmers' market, helping Irene.

Mathew listened attentively, occasionally interrupting to ask an insightful question.

The waiter brought their appetizer and set it in the center of the table.

Pam continued her story, her pride in her mother's success taking center stage.

Mathew smeared a toasted crostini with the creamy cheese and topped it with a slice of tomato. He popped it into his mouth.

Pam paused and watched his face anxiously. "Well? Do you like it?"

"I most certainly do. This is delicious." He grinned at her. "You better dig in, or I'm going to keep you talking while I polish it all off myself."

Pam assembled a crostini for herself. "In that case, I think I'd better ask you a question. I know you work for a bank, but I don't know what you do for them."

"I'm a community banker. I help locally owned businesses with their banking needs—both depository and lending."

"So, you're like an honest-to-goodness banker? The kind of person you hear about in old movies when people say they are going to talk to their banker? Like George Bailey in *A Wonderful Life*?"

Mathew chuckled. "I'm not sure about that—but yes. I get to know my customers' businesses and try to offer them banking advice that will help them grow and prosper."

"That sounds very...noble."

Mathew's shoulders straightened. "That's why I have so much respect for what your mother's doing. I talk with owners of small businesses every day. It's a ton of work to make a living that way. Having a great product—like your mother's handmade aprons and linens—is only a small part of the equation. She has to be a salesperson, marketing director, inventory control manager, bookkeeper, and production supervisor. It sounds like she's mastered all of these."

"She certainly has. She works very hard." Pam found herself warming to this man. "I'm extremely proud of her."

"It's also nice of you to dedicate your Saturday mornings to her—especially since you've worked all week. Your bio says that you're a personal trainer. You're an entrepreneur, too."

The waiter cleared the empty appetizer plate and put artfully arranged plates of sea bass on risotto in front of each of them. They were halfway through their entrees and engaged in a congenial debate over the merits of yoga classes when a fashionable woman in her early forties walked up to their table.

"Mathew," the woman cried warmly. "It's so good to see you!"

Mathew jerked his head in her direction and choked on his sea bass. "Phyllis," he said, attempting to rise from his seat.

"Don't get up," she insisted. "I'm so surprised to see you way over here. I didn't know you ever came to Linden Falls." Phyllis swiveled to face Pam.

"Phyllis, this is Pam. She's...she's a work colleague of mine."

Pam swiveled to face him. A work colleague?

"That explains why you're so far from home," Phyllis said. She gave Pam the once-over with her eyes. "Nice to meet you."

Pam murmured the expected response and swallowed hard. Mathew had that deer-in-the-headlights look. Something was definitely wrong.

"I've heard so much about this place that I had to try it." She spun back to Pam. "How's the food?"

"Fabulous," Pam said, dabbing the corners of her mouth with her napkin. "The sea bass is the best entree I've had in years."

Phyllis nodded as Mathew took a drink from his water glass. "Maybe you and Kathy and Rex and I can come here some Saturday night. We've been meaning to call you. We had such a good time at your barbecue this summer."

Mathew began to sputter and cough. "Sorry," he said, covering his mouth with his hand. "Went down the wrong way."

"I'll let the two of you...get back to it," Phyllis said. "Nice to meet you, Pam. I'll call Kathy next week to get something on our calendars." Phyllis turned on her heel and walked away.

Pam set her knife and fork on her plate, signaling

that she was done. She leaned back in her chair and stared at Mathew.

He rested his elbows on the table and brought his hands to his forehead.

She noticed the telltale indentation on his left ring finger. A wedding ring had recently resided there.

"You're married," she said quietly.

He nodded, keeping his eyes on the table.

"Then why in the *hell* are you here with me?"

He looked at her.

"Why are you on a dating site?"

"I'm not happy in my marriage. Haven't been for years."

"Are you getting a divorce?"

He shrugged.

"What does that mean?"

"I…I don't know. Maybe. I'm just not sure."

"So, this"—she gestured across the table with her upturned hand—"is your attempt to see if you want to leave your wife? Are you shopping around to find out if there's anyone better out there?" Her tone carried a sharp edge.

He cringed. "I wouldn't put it that way."

"Then how would you describe what we're doing here?"

"Just two people…getting to know each other?"

"That's complete bullshit," she hissed. "You lied on your profile. You knew I was coming here on a date." She lunged for her purse at her feet and pulled it onto her lap, rummaging in it for her wallet.

"You're great, Pam. I haven't felt this...alive...in years. You're exactly the kind of woman I want."

"What am I—a new car that you've test-driven, and now you're ready to trade in the old model?" Her voice rose, and people at the neighboring tables began to look their way. Pam pulled three twenty-dollar bills out of her wallet and threw them on the table between them.

"You don't have to do that," Mathew said.

"I'm not about to accept anything from you."

"Can I call you? I'd like to see you again."

"Are. You. Kidding. Me?"

Their waiter began making his way to their table from the other side of the restaurant.

"What about if I've filed for divorce? Can I call you then?"

Pam stood, tipping her chair back.

The waiter caught it before it hit the ground.

"No, Mathew," Pam said. "I don't ever want to hear from you again." She snatched her coat from the back of the chair, squared her shoulders, and strode out of the restaurant.

CHAPTER 12

*P*am pushed against the trainers' break room door just as it opened from the other side. She lurched forward, colliding with Steve, who was just stepping into the room. Her purse slid off her shoulder and fell to the floor.

He put his arms up, grasping her elbows as he steadied her on her feet. "Sorry about that," he said.

Pam regained her footing with an embarrassed chuckle.

Steve bent and picked up her purse. "Are you in a hurry to get out of here to start cooking for tomorrow?"

Pam shook her head. "Mom's taking care of Thanksgiving dinner. It'll just be the two of us. I'm bringing a salad, which I'll throw together in the morning." She positioned her purse strap securely on her shoulder. "What're you doing for Thanksgiving?"

"My sister's taken over hosting duties. My parents

will be there, of course. Everybody brings something." He pointed to the plain paper bag on the table by the coffeepot. "I'm always assigned to bring pies. You wouldn't want anything I tried to make, so I buy them."

Pam stepped aside so he could enter the room.

"Do you have plans tonight?" Steve asked, moving to his locker and retrieving his jacket.

"Not really. I thought I'd go home and veg in front of the TV. How about you?"

"I recorded a couple of college football games. I plan to pick up a pizza and fast-forward through the games."

"Don't you already know who won?"

"Yes." He shrugged as he grabbed the bag with his pies. "I still want to see them play."

They made their way through the empty lobby of the health club to the front door.

"It's only three o'clock," Steve said. "A little early to pick up dinner. I thought I'd check on the toy collection boxes along the square."

"Good idea," Pam said. "That's where we've been getting most of our donations—especially since that day last week when toys started rolling in."

He held the glass door open for her. "I know. It's like someone heard us talking about the lack of donations and decided to fix that."

Pam stepped out into the bright fall afternoon. The temperature was nippy, despite the brilliant sunshine. She wound her scarf around her neck. "I stopped in Duncan's Hardware yesterday afternoon for some plumber's putty. Their collection box was overflowing. I meant to ask you if we should start gathering the toys?"

"I think the collection sites enjoy seeing the mound of toys grow, but you make a good point. We don't want the toys to be in their way. I'll ask them."

"Mind if I tag along?"

"Not at all," Steve said as he headed to his truck. "I'll meet you outside Town Square Books. We'll make the rounds from there."

Pam gave an exaggerated thumbs-up sign and sprinted to her car.

⫸⫸⫸

NEVA OFFERED two women seated at the table by the window another set of pumpkin spice scones. Afternoon tea was always busy the day before Thanksgiving, and she was doubly glad to have Carly's help in the kitchen. She scanned the room. Every table was filled, and all of her guests seemed to be enjoying themselves.

She sighed heavily as she made her way to her office. She'd been ignoring the familiar feeling all afternoon but if there was one thing in life she was sure of, it was to pay attention to this feeling. Neva retrieved her coat, scarf, and purse from the hook behind the door and walked to the kitchen as she thrust her arms into the sleeves.

She grimaced when she stepped inside and found Carly and her mother, Janie, racing from one end of the room to the other. They were either attending to the needs of the afternoon's tea or were preparing for the expected diners at tomorrow's Thanksgiving dinner. Reservations had closed two weeks earlier. For the first time since she'd operated the inn, they were completely booked.

Neva's throat constricted, but she knew what had to be done. She picked up a spoon and tapped it against a water glass.

The mother and daughter stopped in their tracks and turned their eyes to her.

"I have to run out for a minute." She watched as the two sets of eyes widened in unison. "I think everyone in the tea room has what they need—for now. Janie," she addressed the mother, "can you keep an eye on things for me?"

"Of course," Janie said, "but what's so urgent that you have to go out"—Janie held up her palms—"now? If there's something you need, can't it wait?"

Neva shook her head. "I'll be back in a jiffy." She turned on her heel and raced to the front door before Janie could ask her where she was going. The last thing Neva wanted to do was tell the girls she was headed to Town Square Books—and that she didn't know what she needed from there, but she knew it was urgent.

Neva cut across the square, passing the Wishing Tree as she went. She smiled as she noted a slew of new wishes tied to its branches. The weather was predicted to be mild, so she didn't have to worry about getting them off the tree and into the safety of one of her binders. She put her head down and kept going, rustling her feet through the generous carpet of dry leaves on the ground.

The bell above the door tinkled merrily when Neva entered the shop, which was deserted except for the high school girl on duty behind the register. Neva nodded toward her as she stepped inside, but the girl was engrossed in something on her phone and didn't look up.

Neva approached a round table containing a display of cookbooks. She had more cookbooks than her shelves could hold, but the table drew her to it. She was perusing the titles and admiring the glossy photos of perfectly staged culinary creations when the door opened, admitting a blast of chilly air together with Steve and Pam.

"Neva," Pam cried, rushing to the older woman and giving her a quick hug. "What are you doing here?"

Neva looked between the two of them and realized she now had her answer. She dropped her hand to the table and picked up the book it landed on. "I'm doing some Christmas shopping," she said, holding up the latest reprint of the classic *Mastering the Art of French Cooking.*

"I tried some of the recipes from my mom's copy," Pam said. "It was way too advanced for my skill level."

"It's not for everybody, that's for sure." She reached over and patted Pam's arm. "I'm going to give it to Carly. Her mother works for me at the inn, and Carly has become invaluable in the kitchen. She's quite a cook and dreams of going to culinary school in France. I'm hoping to pour a little Miracle-Gro on that dream."

"That's nice of you," Steve said.

"So, what brings the two of you in here this afternoon?"

"We're checking on the toy collection boxes," he replied.

"I look in the window at the café almost every day. Those toys are starting to pile up. It makes me so happy to see them." She turned to Pam while watching Steve out of the corner of her eye. "How's the dating going?"

Pam rolled her eyes. "You don't want to know."

Neva cocked an eyebrow that signaled she did want to know.

"I've had two dates—both disasters."

"Oh?"

"One did nothing but complain the entire time, and the other was an attractive man who'd concealed the fact that he was married."

"That's not good. But two dates are hardly enough for you to draw any conclusions."

"I know." Pam held up her hand in a stop sign gesture. "I promised you and my mom that I'd give this dating site a thirty-day trial."

Steve took a step back and looked away.

"I'm going out one more time on Sunday," Pam said, unable to keep the dejection out of her voice. She just wanted it to be over with, and then, hopefully, her mother—and Neva—would let it go and leave her be.

Steve's lips flattened into a line, and he walked over to the collection box.

Neva smiled inwardly. The thought of Pam going out with another man bothered Steve. She was sure of it. "Well, you know what they say: third time's the charm." She stepped to the counter and handed the cookbook to the girl, who was forced to tear her attention away from her phone. "I'd better get back to the inn. We're crazy busy right now." She handed her credit card to the teen. "You two have a lovely Thanksgiving. And good luck on your date." Neva took her card and package from the teen and exited the shop.

"Thank you. I hope you have a nice holiday, too," Pam called after her.

"The box is only half-full," Steve said as Pam joined him. "We don't need to haul anything away from here."

"Agreed," Pam said, leaning over to poke through the donated items. "They're all books." She pulled out a Nancy Drew and ran her hand across the cover. "Gosh, I devoured the whole series. I wanted to be Nancy, with her blue roadster and her independence."

Steve chuckled. "I think you turned out pretty independent, but a Prius isn't a roadster," he teased.

"I guess not. I love my car, but after seeing this"— she held the book aloft—"I may need to trade it in." She replaced the Nancy Drew in the box. "There are a lot of books in this box. I'm pleased."

"On to the next?" Steve swept his arm to the door.

"Lead on," she said. "Any boxes we don't get to today, I can check on Saturday."

"Won't you be too busy getting ready for your big date?"

"It's not a 'big date,' and I'm going to Duncan's Hardware on Saturday morning to buy paint, anyway. I'm planning to paint an accent wall in my bedroom this weekend."

Steve nodded as they turned into the wind and walked the block to the Crooked Porch Café. "Well, I hope this one is better than the other two."

"What?" Pam asked, leaning toward him and pulling her scarf away from her ear.

"Your date." Steve raised his voice above the wind and leaned close to her. "Good luck."

Pam nodded. "Thank you. Based on my recent experiences, I'm not expecting much. My thirty-day trial is over this weekend. I fully expect to be joining you in the no-dating pledge on Monday." She pulled her scarf up over her ears again and didn't see the smile spread across Steve's face.

CHAPTER 13

"Uncle Steve!" Ben cried, throwing his arms around his favorite uncle's waist as Steve crossed his sister's threshold.

"Hey, buddy," Steve said. "Let me put these pies in the kitchen. If I drop them, your mother's gonna kill me."

Ben released his death grip on his uncle. "Can we go outside and play football?"

"Of course. What else would we do while the turkey is in the oven? Go get your brother and sister and put your coats on. It's cold out there. I'll meet you in the backyard."

"Yeah!" Ben turned to the family room, hollering, "Riley! Emma! Uncle Steve's going to play football with us."

Sugar, his sister's golden retriever, opened one eye and got slowly to her feet. At eleven, she preferred her cozy spot in the swath of sunshine on the family room carpet, but her sense of duty compelled her to follow the children outside.

Steve stepped into the kitchen. Steam fogged the window over the sink, and every available surface was covered with pots, pans, and cooking utensils.

Carol stood at the open oven door, turkey baster in hand. "Thank goodness you're here," she said, her eyes remaining focused on her basting of the oversized bird.

"That looks—and smells—great already." He glanced at the disaster scene that was the kitchen. "Where would you like the pies?"

Carol closed the oven door and removed her quilted mitts. "Wherever you can find room," she said curtly.

Steve began clearing a spot near the sink for his carrier bag with the pies.

"Not there," Carol snapped. "That's where I'll put clean dishes. If I ever get a chance to start cleaning up some of this mess."

Steve quickly removed his bag. "Are you doing this all by yourself?"

Carol slumped against the counter and nodded. "Mom's arthritis is flaring, so she and Dad aren't coming until right before dinner and Tom's at the hospital."

"I thought he had the day off."

"We did, too, but one of the other ER doctors was in a car accident last night. It's nothing serious, but he can't work, so Tom had to cover his shift. ERs are busy on holidays. He couldn't leave them short-staffed. His shift is over at three, so he'll be home for dinner."

"Sounds like he didn't have a choice, but I'm sorry that leaves you in the lurch. Why didn't you call me? I could have come over earlier."

Carol shrugged. "I thought I could handle it. And I could have if the kids hadn't been such a handful. Bickering over the most trivial things all morning." She pulled her damp hair off of her face and secured it into a ponytail using an elastic band she fished out of the pocket of her jeans. "I'm glad you're here. They've been so wound up, thinking about throwing the football around with you—their famous uncle who played in the NFL."

"I don't know how famous playing two games in the NFL makes me. I had one of the shortest pro careers ever." He surveyed the kitchen. "Tell you what," he said. "I'll get the kids started running sprints and I'll come back in here to wash dishes."

"You don't have to do that. I can manage." Carol said the words without conviction.

"Nonsense. I'll wash, and you can dry. What is it you say from the bench? *Order in the court*? We're going to restore order in the kitchen."

Carol laughed. "I actually never say that from the bench, but I'd be grateful for your help."

"I smell coffee. Would you pour me a cup, and I'll go wrangle the kids?"

"Deal," she said, her shoulders rising.

"Be right back." Steve hurried to the backyard, and his nephews, ages ten and twelve, and his eight-year-old niece flocked to him. As Sugar settled in a sunny spot in the yard, Steve walked the kids through a course that wove around the outdoor grill and through the patio furniture, now covered in heavy canvas for the upcoming winter. "When you're done with ten repetitions of that, you can run sprints around the perimeter of the yard. That's how the pros warm up." He was glad they weren't old enough to know better. "I'm going to help your mom with the dishes, and I'll come out to throw passes to you when we're done."

"Awww...we thought we were gonna play with you now," Emma whined.

"If you want to come inside with me and help in the kitchen, that'll make it go faster," Steve said.

"No. That's okay," Riley said quickly. "We'll get warmed up like you said."

Steve brought his hands together and rubbed them. "Off you go. Give me your best. I'll be back in a jiffy."

The kids scattered.

"And no fighting!" Steve called on his way to the back door. "That'll get you thrown out of the game." He patted Sugar on the top of her head and rejoined Carol in the kitchen.

She moved away from the breakfast room window, where she'd been watching the scene in the backyard. Carol handed Steve a steaming mug of coffee.

"Thanks." He raised the mug to his lips and inhaled. "Is there cinnamon in this?"

Carol nodded. "Just the way you like it."

"You spoil me."

"Somebody should," she said. "You deserve so much more, Steve."

They crossed to the sink, and Steve inserted the stopper and squeezed a big dollop of dishwashing liquid into the stream of hot water. "You say that because I'm your brother—the one who's about to wash your dishes."

Carol flicked his backside with a towel. "I'm saying that because it's true. Having your football career ended by that stupid injury during your second game was nothing short of tragic. It was a dirty hit—you'll never convince me otherwise." She took the pan he handed her and rubbed it vigorously with the dish towel. "Then that self-centered, shallow-minded, pea-brained wife of yours—"

"How did you really feel about her?" Steve interrupted.

"Walks out on you while you're still in the hospital? I'll never forgive her for that."

"I was pretty upset at the time…"

"You were devastated."

"But I've come to realize that she did me a favor. Jenna was never interested in anyone but herself. She was gorgeous—but only on the outside. Mom and Dad showed us what a real marriage looks like." He glanced at his sister. "You and Tom got it right, too. The fact that I made such a poor choice is on me."

Carol pursed her lips. "Jenna could put on quite a show when she wanted to. Mom and Dad and I all liked her at first. Don't blame yourself."

Steve shrugged as he continued whittling down the stack of dirty dishes. "Water over the dam now."

Carol rested her hands on the counter and faced him. "Except it's not 'over.' You're not moving on with your life. I watch you with my three—you're so good with them. You'd make a wonderful dad. And I know you want kids."

He shook his head and held up a hand to stop her.

"You can't fool me, Steve."

"Look, I've tried, okay? I've dated dozens of women since my divorce. I've even gotten close to a couple of them. And all of my relationships have ended badly."

"You've just picked the wrong women."

He spun on her. "I agree. I have. I can't seem to pick out someone I can be happy with." His words came faster. "After each failed relationship, I've been more discouraged than before. Not to mention the misery and loneliness I felt during the process. I've finally realized that I'm better off on my own."

They stared at each other.

"I'd love to have a happy marriage—like you or our parents have—but I'm just not lucky in love. I can't keep torturing myself, going on blind dates or searching through dating websites. It was sucking the life out of me." He sighed heavily. "I'm fine as I am. Isn't that good enough for you?"

Carol leaned over and drew him into a hug. "All I want is for my baby brother to be happy," she said, her voice thick with emotion. "Don't give up, okay? Keep your eyes open. Your soul mate may be right in front of you. You don't want to miss her."

CHAPTER 14

*P*am set the painter's tape on the floor. She'd finished prepping the accent wall in her bedroom. If she rolled the paint—in the warm brown tone happily named Graham Cracker—now, it would be dry by bedtime, and she could move her bed back into place.

She checked her clock and groaned. She didn't have time. Why in the world had she agreed to meet Cyrus Clemmons for coffee in the middle of her Sunday afternoon?

She gazed wistfully at the can of paint that sat on the tarp in the middle of her bedroom floor. She'd planned to paint this wall yesterday afternoon but had been too tired. The last farmers' market of the season had been packed, and Irene had kept her booth open for an extra hour and a half. The memory of her mother's excitement at having sold almost all of her inventory filled Pam's heart. Her mother deserved every ounce of success she worked so hard for.

They'd celebrated the conclusion of the most successful season Irene had had since she'd taken a booth at the market with an early dinner at the Crooked Porch Café. She'd helped her mother store the booth in the back of Irene's garage, where it would stay until it would be needed when the market resumed in the spring. When she'd finally made it home, she'd crawled into bed with Leopold and a book—and been sound asleep before she'd finished the next chapter.

Pam hesitated, toying with the idea of postponing her rendezvous. Completing this task was sorely tempting. She glanced at the clock again and forced herself to move toward her bathroom. It was too late to change plans now. Cyrus would undoubtedly be on the way to the coffeeshop—if he wasn't there already.

Pam toed off her old sneakers while she swiped her cheeks with blush. She glanced at her jeans and T-shirt, glad that she hadn't yet started to paint. The T-shirt was a bit clingier than she liked but was presentable enough to go out in. She removed her hair tie and shook out her chestnut mane around her shoulders. She shoved her feet into her favorite heeled dress boots and closed the zippers. She raced to her door and snatched her jacket and purse from their hooks.

Leopold followed, close on her heels, meowing plaintively.

"I'll feed you when I get home. I won't be gone long," she said as she opened the door.

Leopold turned up the volume.

"This is probably the last date I'm going to have for a while. I'm at the end of the thirty-day trial of this online dating site. So, unless this guy is seriously great, I'm done."

Leopold screeched loudly.

"You're fine," Pam said, closing the door on him.

She drove to the nearby coffeeshop as fast as she could and was relieved to find a parking spot right in front. She took a deep breath before she got out of her car. It wasn't Cyrus's fault that she'd rather be home, painting her bedroom wall. She needed to put a smile on her face and be good company for this man who was also interrupting his Sunday afternoon to meet a stranger—her—in a coffeeshop. Online dating wasn't easy for anyone.

Pam stepped into the shop, and the aroma of strong coffee enveloped her. The milk frother was whirring away. A long line of customers waiting to place their orders wound around the right side of the shop. She scanned the people seated at tables tucked into every available nook and cranny. There was only one table occupied by a sole man. Her heart sank.

The man had already spotted her and was waving.

She nodded in acknowledgment and wove her way through the crowded space to him.

He stood as she approached his table. Short and stocky, he wore bright red jeans and a button-down shirt in a vibrant patchwork of red, yellow, and green squares. Completing his ensemble was a green-and-yellow-striped bow tie.

Her eyes widened as she got close, and she wondered if it would be rude to put on her sunglasses. Even in the dim interior of the coffeeshop, his attire seemed to glow.

An older man at an adjoining table looked between Pam and Cyrus. His eyebrows shot up, and Pam swore she could see pity in the man's expression.

"Cyrus Clemmons," he said, straightening his bow tie. "You must be Pam Olson?"

She nodded and slipped into the chair opposite him.

"I'm so sorry I'm late," Pam said. "I was involved in a painting project at my house and lost track of time. Have you been here long?"

"Fifteen minutes. I was early. I had a gig and came here right afterward so I wouldn't be late."

"Now I really feel bad," Pam said. "What kind of gig?"

"I'm a magician," Cyrus said. "I had a kid's birthday party before this."

"That's right," Pam said, bringing her hand to her forehead. "I remember reading that in your profile. It's one of your hobbies."

"More like my obsession," he said. "I'm hoping to make it big one day."

"That's why you're wearing…" she began, stopping abruptly at the puzzled look on his face. "So…what would 'making it big' look like for you?"

"I'd have an act in Vegas."

"Like Penn and Teller?"

"Exactly."

"Have you been there to see their show?"

He shook his head. "Not yet, but it's on my bucket list." He leaned over and put a hand by her ear. "Do you mind? You have something stuck back here." He withdrew his hand and pulled out a quarter. "I thought so," he said, handing it to her.

Pam laughed. "My grandfather used to pull quarters out of my ears all the time when I was little. I loved it. Did you do that at your party earlier?"

Cyrus nodded.

"What else is part of your act?"

"The usual card tricks and making stuff disappear." He sighed heavily.

"What fun! I've always found it fascinating to see magicians work. I can never figure out how they do their tricks."

"Then you haven't gone on YouTube to find out. Kids have seen it all."

"Hmmm…that must make things hard for you. What's your best crowd-pleaser?"

"Funny you should ask," Cyrus said. "I hope you don't mind, but I've got him here with me. The entire time we were waiting, he was telling me he wanted to meet you."

Pam cocked her head to one side as Cyrus fumbled in the satchel tucked under his chair. He brought out a ventriloquist dummy, attired in an outfit and blond crew cut that matched Cyrus. She looked from one to the other. The effect was arresting.

A little boy at the table to Cyrus's right squirmed in his chair to get a better look at the colorful pair.

Cyrus positioned the dummy over his arm, with Clyde's feet propped up on the table. "Clyde, I'd like you to meet my date—Miss Pam Olson."

"Hubba hubba!" the dummy said.

"What...?" Pam began.

"He just gets excited sometimes," Cyrus said.

Clyde swiveled to the small boy and winked.

The boy smiled and gave them his full attention.

"Wasn't Edgar Bergen famous for being a ventriloquist?" Pam asked.

"He sure was. Nobody our age or younger knows that anymore. I'm impressed." Cyrus gave her a full-toothed smile. "His friend's name was Charlie McCarthy."

Pam brought her hand to her head. "Thank you. I was racking my brain, trying to remember the name of his dum...er...character," she said, noticing in time the look of horror on Cyrus's face as she started to say the word *dummy*. She leaned over the table, giving Clyde her full attention.

"Look at that rack!" Clyde erupted in a loud voice.

Pam recoiled in her chair.

The young boy's mother frowned at Cyrus and scooted her son's chair away from the foul-mouthed dummy.

"Manners, Clyde. You don't want to offend our guest." Cyrus looked up at Pam. "Sorry about that."

Pam glanced to her left. The mother of the small boy was staring at them disapprovingly.

Cyrus took a sip of his coffee.

Clyde looked up at Cyrus and nodded to get his attention.

Cyrus bent over and put his ear close to Clyde. "I wonder how long it'll take you to get to third base with this one," Clyde said in a stage whisper.

"Now that's enough," Cyrus said. "He has no filter…"

Pam gasped, wondering if she'd heard correctly. The shocked look on the mother's face at the adjacent table told her she had. Pam jumped to her feet and pulled her purse onto her shoulder.

"Are you going to get yourself a coffee?" Cyrus asked.

"No. I…I think I'd better go."

Cyrus lunged toward her and grabbed for her hand. "Is it Clyde? It is, isn't it? I can leave him home next time."

"No." Pam pulled her hand away. "I don't think… There's not going to be a next time."

"But we…I…haven't learned anything about you yet. We'd like to, wouldn't we, Clyde?"

"There's a lot I'd like to know about you, doll," Clyde said.

Pam took a step away from the table, searching for something polite to say. "Good luck with your career. I hope your Vegas dreams come true." Then, not giving him a chance to respond, she turned on her heel and fled out of the coffeeshop without a backward glance.

By the time she was halfway home, she had made two decisions: this would be her last match from the online dating service, and she had time to paint her accent wall.

CHAPTER 15

$\mathscr{P}$am was pulling on her gloves as she strode across the lobby of Linden Falls Fitness when she heard Steve call her name.

"Where're you headed in such a screaming hurry?"

"Duncan's Hardware," she replied, stopping with one hand on the door. "I was there on Saturday morning, buying paint. The collection box was overflowing and spilling into the aisle. Jed Duncan said he doesn't have anywhere to store the extra toys, so I offered to pick them up today. All the toys come back here for sorting, anyway. We can add them to our display." She pointed over her shoulder to the mound of toys along the far wall.

"Good thinking. Why didn't you ask me to help?"

"You always have a full morning of clients on Mondays. I figured you'd be busy." She leaned against the door to open it. "I have an hour and a half between clients, so I have plenty of time."

"As a matter of fact, I don't have anyone again until noon. Most of my Monday morning people went out of town for Thanksgiving and aren't home yet. Let me grab my jacket, and I'll join you." He sprinted toward the stairs to the second floor without waiting for her answer.

"I'll bring my car around and pick you up at the door," she called after him.

Steve emerged from the building as she pulled to the curb. "I don't think we've ever had so many toys that we've had to make an early pickup. I'll bet this'll be a record-breaking year."

They glanced at each other and grinned.

"So…how was your Thanksgiving?" Steve asked.

"Nice. Very quiet. Mom's a fabulous cook, and she made a huge turkey so that we both had enough leftovers to last all weekend. I spent the rest of my time working on my house." She put on her blinker and turned onto the road. "How about you?"

"I always have fun at my sister's. Her kids are a handful, but they're great. I'm lucky to have such a close-knit family."

Pam drove toward the square.

"So…you painted something? With the paint you bought at Duncan's?"

Pam nodded. "An accent wall. It came out great." She launched into a description of the color and how it brought out the undertones of the artwork above her bed.

Steve nodded and *aha*-ed as if he were paying attention. He wanted her to talk about her date on Saturday. He seized his moment when she paused to concentrate on parallel parking in front of the hardware store. "Did you do anything else, or did you stay in the house all weekend?"

Pam put her car into park and reached into the back seat for her purse. "I had another date with a man from the online dating service." She got out of the car.

"Oh?" Steve leaped out on his side. "Nice guy?"

Pam rolled her eyes as she came around the car to him. "You wouldn't believe me if I told you."

"Try me."

"Maybe when we have more time." She pointed to the door emblazoned with the words *Duncan's Hardware*. "Right now, we need to clear the toys out of Jed's aisles."

Pam and Steve spent the next ten minutes ferrying toys from the store to her Prius. Jed joined them for the final load.

"Thanks for doing this, guys," he said. "We're renovating our storage areas in back and don't have room this year to store these." He picked up an armload of toys and followed Pam and Steve to her car.

"I'm amazed that you've gotten all of these toys into *this* car," Jed said.

"You should see her in action, packing this thing," Steve said, gesturing to Pam with his head. "She's a master at filling up every space."

"She certainly is," Jed said, handing toys to Pam so

she could stow them. "Oh...I almost forgot." He brought his palm to his temple. "Neva called right before you arrived and asked me to send you over to the inn when you're done here."

Pam stopped rearranging toys and turned to him. "How did she know we'd be here?"

"I figured you must have told her," Jed said.

Pam and Jed looked at Steve.

Steve shrugged. "It wasn't me. I didn't know, myself, that I'd be coming here today until right before we left the gym."

"Well...it's Neva. She knows stuff that the rest of us don't," Jed said.

"You can say that again," Steve mumbled.

"What does she want to see us about?" Pam asked.

"She didn't say," Jed replied. "Whatever it is, I'm sure it's important. You'd better get over there."

>»))

NEVA THREW OPEN the door of the inn as Pam and Steve mounted the top step. "Good morning," she said with robust good cheer. "Thank you for stopping by."

They entered the foyer, and Neva started down the long hallway, gesturing for them to follow her. She opened the door to her private sitting room and ushered them inside.

"What...what do you need, Neva? What're we doing here?" Pam asked.

Neva motioned them into the wing chairs that flanked the hearth. A cozy fire flickered behind the grate. Sun streamed in the window, creating a checkered pattern on the rich Aubusson carpet on the floor.

"Do you need help with the toys in your collection box?" Steve asked.

Neva shook her head. "We're collecting a ton of toys this year, but there's plenty of room for them all."

"Then...why did you tell Jed you needed to see us?"

"I woke up this morning with the strongest feeling that the two of you needed to come here"—she paused, looking between the two quizzical expressions directed at her—"and have tea," she finished in a rush.

Steve jerked back in his chair.

Pam cocked her head to one side. "Really?"

Neva reached for the doorknob. "I'll go get the tea. The two of you are here because you need to talk." She turned the handle and disappeared down the hall.

Pam shook her head and stared, wide-eyed, after her. "I've heard stories about Neva's weird, clairvoyant tendencies, but this takes the cake." She stood.

The aroma of freshly baked muffins filtered into the room.

Pam sat back down.

"We have time, and I'm starved," Steve said. "Why don't we have tea and muffins? After all, it'll make Neva happy."

"If you put it that way, I guess you're right."

"You can tell me the tale of your date."

Pam grimaced. "I'm not sure I want to."

Neva glided into the room with a tea tray and a plate of cranberry muffins, warm from the oven. "Forgive me for eavesdropping," she said. "I heard what you said as I was coming down the hall. Sometimes it's good to talk about things that disappointed us." She poured two cups of tea and dosed each with an extra-large dollop of lavender honey. Neva handed a cup to Pam and then to Steve. "Take your time and enjoy yourselves. The room is yours for as long as you need it." She exited the room as quickly as she'd entered it.

"She's weird but so nice," Pam said.

"Agreed." Steve took a bite of one of the muffins. "You've got to try these. They're amazing." He washed it down with a sip of the tea. "I think Neva's right. It's therapeutic to talk."

"You have to promise not to tease me about this."

He raised his hand with three extended fingers. "Scout's honor."

"Okay...have you ever heard of the ventriloquist Edgar Bergen?"

Steve's brow furrowed. "Wasn't his dummy named Charlie McCarthy?"

"Very good." She leaned forward in her chair, balancing her teacup on her knee. "Imagine having a blind date—with both of them."

Steve's eyes widened. "Seriously? Gosh, I've got to hear about this."

Pam launched into a detailed description of the date she'd hoped she would forget. When she came to the part where Clyde had wondered if Cyrus would get to third base, Steve had to clamp his hand over his mouth to keep himself from laughing aloud.

Pam gave him a stern look, then burst out laughing herself.

Steve removed his hand and joined her.

"I was astounded, annoyed, and embarrassed, all at the same time. People at nearby tables were staring. It was humiliating."

"That must have been awful," Steve said.

"It was. I couldn't beat feet out of there fast enough."

"I can imagine. It's funny now, but I know from experience how depressed that kind of thing can make you feel."

"Exactly! I was so glad I had that wall to paint when I got home. It took my mind off of things, but I was out of sorts all weekend."

"Yep. Been there, done that." He finished his muffin. "Is your thirty-day trial of online dating completed?'

Pam nodded.

"And on the whole, are you feeling better, happier, and less alone than before you started the trial?"

"That's an easy one to answer—no, no, and definitely not."

Steve leaned toward her. "Are you ready?"

She drained her teacup. "For the no-dating pledge?"

He nodded.

"More than ready. How should we memorialize it? Do we pinky swear?"

"Pinky swearing is for kids." He raised his right

hand, motioning for her to follow suit. "Repeat after me: I…"

"I."

"Do…"

"Do."

"Not…"

"Not."

"Date…"

"Date."

"No reservations and no exceptions…"

Pam grinned and repeated the last phrase.

Steve lowered his right hand and held it out to her.

She shook it. They smiled into each other's eyes. "How will this work?" she asked.

"We encourage each other to stick to the pledge." His tone was light, but his words were serious. "This is about our sense of self-worth. If there's one thing I've learned, it's that it's my responsibility to make myself happy. If dating doesn't make me happy, then I get to choose not to do it. No matter how much other people try to push me."

"They only want what's best for us."

"Of course they do. But they're not living our lives. We get to decide what makes us happy."

"That whole online dating thing didn't work for me."

"Then it's perfectly reasonable to stop doing it."

Pam felt something against her legs and looked down to see Neva's cat Charm winding around her ankles. She stared at her a moment before looking back up at Steve. "But can I tell you a secret? Sometimes, I think I'd like to find someone to share my life with."

"Sometimes, I do, too. But online dating and blind dates set up by friends or family haven't worked out for me. I end up feeling miserable. I've accepted the fact that my life is fine as it is."

The doorknob turned, and Neva swept into the room, a Cheshire-cat grin playing at her lips.

Pam wondered if she'd been listening on the other side of the door.

"I see you've finished your tea and muffins. Would you like some more?"

Pam checked her watch. "No, thanks. We've both got to get back to the gym."

Steve pulled out his wallet and began removing a credit card.

Neva put out a hand to stop him. "My treat."

He held the card out to her. "You don't have to do that."

"I want to do it."

Pam and Steve got to their feet.

"Those muffins were fabulous, and there was something awfully comforting about that tea," Steve said. He drew Neva to him in a one-armed hug.

"Thank you, Neva," Pam said. "We're usually booked solid all day long. It was so nice to sit and have a treat in the middle of the morning."

"You're most welcome," Neva said, leading them through the foyer. She stood in the open doorway and watched the pair walk to Pam's car. She glanced at the

Wishing Tree as the clouds parted, and a ray of sunshine traced the outline of its leafless branches.

The Prius pulled away from the curb and, for a split second, was embraced by the sunshine that had already hugged the Wishing Tree.

Neva's heart soared. It was a good omen if ever she'd seen one.

CHAPTER 16

*S*teve turned and used his back to open the door to the workout room where they'd moved the toys for sorting. "This is the last load," he said to Pam, holding out the armful of boxes before he added them to the mound in the middle of the room. "We're lucky that Fran canceled her Saturday morning Zumba class so that we could use this room."

Pam nodded and continued taping signs on the wall. "I've got Dolls, Action Figures, Games & Puzzles, Cars, Legos, Balls, Bikes, Electronics, and Arts & Crafts," she said, pointing around the room. "We'll separate the toys into categories and then sort them into age brackets within each group."

"Excellent." Steve surveyed the scene in front of him. "We've got our work cut out for us."

"I forgot to tell you," Pam said. "Brian and Barb are coming here around ten to help us. They have to leave by noon to get ready for their annual Christmas party tonight, but she said they'd be running errands this morning and could spare a couple of hours."

"That's super. We could use the help. I'll bet we've collected double what we got last year."

"That's incredible!" She joined him in the center of the room and hugged herself. "It's so much fun to see this stuff. I played with some of these toys when I was a kid. Brings back memories."

"That it does. I was into Legos. It's nice to see that they're still so popular." He pointed to a large set at the edge of the pile. "What time does the news crew get here?"

"Two. That'll give them time to edit the story before they run it on the six o'clock news."

Pam and Steve turned to each other. "You're doing the interview," they said to each other.

"You've been working on the toy drive for years," Pam said. "I'm a newbie. It's not fair for me to take credit for this. You're the one who should do the talking."

"I do it every year. People are tired of me."

Pam slanted her eyes at him.

"Okay," he said. "I'll be the spokesperson—on one condition. You stand with me and smile at the camera. You'll add beauty and charm to the piece. People at home may actually stop what they're doing to watch."

"It's a deal," Pam said, ignoring the compliment. "We'd better get started." She took a clam-shelled package of watercolor pencils and moved it to the Arts

& Crafts section. "You know what? I'd like a set of these, myself."

"You'll have to tell Santa," Steve said as he got busy sorting toys.

By the time Barb and Brian arrived at ten fifteen, the two trainers were almost halfway through moving toys into their categories.

"Look at all this!" Brian turned in a circle. "And the bikes! How many are there?"

"Two dozen," Steve replied. "In the past, we've only gotten one or two. This has been—by far—our best year."

Barb and Brian smiled at each other.

"I think the early burst of donations primed the pump. Got things going." Steve looked from Barb to Brian. "The two of you wouldn't happen to know anything about that, would you?"

Brian held out his hands, palms up, and shrugged. "Who knows?"

"Thought so." Steve clapped Brian on the back. "The two of you are kind and generous. We're lucky to have you here in Linden Falls."

"We'd better get busy, or we won't be any help to you at all," Barb said, brushing aside the compliment. "What can we do?"

Pam explained their system and they all got busy. By the time Barb declared that they needed to leave, the toys had been moved to their categories and they'd made a good start on separating them into age groups.

"I hate leaving you with the rest of this," Barb said,

"but we need to pick up ice and a few odds and ends before the caterers arrive."

"No worries. We can easily finish by two. The local TV news station is coming to do a news story about this," Pam said, pointing to the neatly arranged piles of toys. "I'll even have time to fix my hair and makeup."

"That's wonderful. I can't get enough good-news stories. When will it air?"

"At six o'clock," Steve said.

Barb clasped her hands together. "I've just had the best idea. Why don't you both come to our party? We'll have the TVs tuned to the local news station. It'll be so much fun for our guests—and for both of you—to see your story air at the party."

Pam and Steve both shook their heads.

"We don't want to crash your party," he said.

"I'm sure you've already given a head count to your caterer," Pam added.

"Nonsense. It's an open house for over a hundred people. We always have a ton of food left over." Barb pressed her hands to the sides of her face. "I'm ashamed that I didn't invite you earlier. I can't imagine what I was thinking. We'd love you to come."

"Anyone who had anything to do with the toy drive would want you to be there," Brian said, looking pointedly at Steve.

"It does sound like fun," Steve said. "I don't have any other plans tonight." He turned to Pam.

"I can make it." She grinned at Barb. "I haven't been to a Christmas party in years."

Barb beamed. "Awesome. Can you be there before six?"

"Sure. Text me your address. Want to ride with me?" Steve asked Pam.

"Good idea," Barb interjected. "Parking will be at a premium."

"Then, yes. I'll go with you. What should we wear?"

Barb's eyes sparkled. "The two of you will be the stars of the show. Plus, you're both gorgeous. You can wear anything, but I'd suggest you pull out all the stops and glam it up."

Pam began to shake her head.

"I like that idea," Steve said. "I haven't been out of gym clothes for weeks. I think it's time for my suit to come out of mothballs." He addressed Pam. "Do you think you can compete with that?"

Pam cuffed his shoulder. "You'll just have to wait and see."

Brian winked at Barb. "We're out of here," he said. "Based on what Steve's just said, I may get my tuxedo out of the back of my closet."

"See you both real soon," Barb said, taking Brian's arm and exiting the classroom.

Pam and Steve got back to work.

As Barb and Brian were getting into their car, she turned to her husband. "Guess where I want to stop on the way home?"

Brian raised his brows as he looked at his wife, digging through her purse for a pen. "Really?"

"You bet. You know I believe in the Wishing Tree."

"But you've already posted this wish."

"There's no law that says you can't make the same wish twice."

"You won't be talked out of this, will you?"

"Nope. Let's get rolling. We've still got a lot to do before the party."

⫸⫸

Pam surveyed herself in the full-length mirror on the back of her closet door. The shimmery red dress with the cowl neckline and body-hugging ruching still fit her like a second skin. The sleeveless dress attractively showcased her toned arms. Her grandmother's wedding diamond, set into a simple pendant, rested at the base of her throat. Kitten heels assured that she'd tolerate being on her feet all evening.

She'd begun getting ready as soon as she'd gotten home at three. She'd arranged her hair on top of her head and taken it down again three different times. She'd settled on letting it hang in loose curls around her shoulders. Viewing herself in the mirror convinced her that she'd made the right choice.

She picked up her evening clutch, turned out the bedroom light, and walked to the front door. Her coat was waiting, folded on the bench inside the door.

Her phone pinged. She read the text from Steve.

Be there in two minutes. Don't come out when you see my truck. I'm coming to the door to get you.

Pam rested the phone against her chin and smiled.

Steve was a gentleman, through and through. She stood at the window and watched him pull into her driveway and then walked toward the front door.

Steve's tall, trim frame was perfectly clothed in an inky navy suit. A white shirt, silver tie, and pocket square completed his ensemble. He looked like he'd been styled for a photo shoot. Her pulse quickened. Lance had been nice-looking, but Steve was hands down the most handsome man she'd ever been out with.

Pam took a step back and brought her hand to her heart. What was she thinking? She wasn't going out with Steve. He was just giving her a ride to a party. That was all there was to it.

The doorbell buzzed and she snatched her coat from the bench as she opened her door.

Steve's eyes traveled the length of her before returning to her face. "Wow," he said. "You look absolutely gorgeous." He took her coat from her and helped her on with it.

"You clean up pretty well, yourself," Pam said.

He put his hand in the small of her back and turned her toward the open door.

She stepped into him as she crossed the threshold. The blood pounded in her ears, and she inhaled deeply. "OMG," she said. "You're wearing aftershave."

"I wanted to make sure I didn't smell like the gym."

"Mission accomplished," she said as they walked to his car. "You smell fabulous. Every woman at this party will want to get close to you."

Steve laughed. "I'm not so sure about that, but I do know that every unmarried guy will be trying to get your number. You look beautiful."

"Thank you."

"It's a good thing we're going with each other. We can keep any interested parties at arm's length."

"Upholding the no-dating pledge?"

"Exactly. We're a team."

"Good to remember. We can relax and enjoy the party."

The party was, as Barb promised, great fun. Food and drink were plentiful. Christmas trees were set out in every room, with a twelve-footer soaring to the ceiling by the staircase. The air was thick with the scent of pine, mingled with the aroma of red roses from a giant arrangement on the dining room table. Laughter emanated from every corner, and Pam was relieved to find Paige standing there when they arrived, making it feel less awkward walking in.

Brian tapped his wineglass to get everyone's attention. "As you may know, Pam Olson and Steve Turner ran this year's toy drive." He gestured to them to join him. "I'm thrilled to announce that it's been the most successful drive in the history of Linden Falls."

Applause ran through the crowd.

"They're going to be on TV, talking about it, in a few minutes," he said, directing the guests to the many television sets that had been set up to show the news story.

Brian tapped his glass again at the end of the

feature. "Please join me in raising your glasses and toasting Pam and Steve's hard work in making this effort such a success. Thanks to them—and our generous community of Linden Falls—a great many children will have something new under the tree this Christmas." He raised his glass. "To Pam and Steve."

The guests raised their glasses. "Hear, hear," reverberated around the room before they all took a sip from their glasses.

Pam and Steve were immediately surrounded by people, shaking their hands and expressing appreciation. By the time they'd each managed to fill a plate and have a bite to eat, the attention from other partygoers had died down.

Steve drifted into the media room to watch a football game playing on the widescreen TV. Pam joined a group of others gathered around the piano in the living room to sing carols. At the end of a rousing version of *Deck the Halls*, she glanced up to find Steve leaning against the doorframe, staring in her direction.

She raised a hand in a tentative wave.

He gave her a thumbs-up sign and made his way to her, bending close so he could hear her above the din.

"You're going to sing with us?"

"I thought I would."

"You're a man of many talents. I didn't know you could sing."

"I can't carry a tune in a bucket, but there's one carol I'm an expert in."

"Now I'm intrigued." Her lips brushed his ear.

"Is the piano player taking requests?"

Pam's hand shot in the air, and she waved it until she got the pianist's attention. "I've got a special request," she said, moving a half step to one side and pointing to Steve. "Not only is this man a TV star, but he's also got a signature Christmas carol to share with us."

"By all means," the piano player said.

Steve made his way to the piano bench. He bent and whispered in the woman's ear. She nodded vigorously and placed her hands on the keys.

Steve cleared his throat and drew himself up to his full height. "It's now my very great pleasure to offer you my rendition of the classic made popular by the king himself—Elvis Presley. I give you 'Blue Christmas.'"

The pianist played a showy introduction, and Steve began the song—in a spot-on impression of Porky Pig.

The group gathered at the piano began to chuckle. By the time Steve finished the second verse, the other partygoers had joined them. Before long, everyone was wheezing with laughter, and the piano player had trouble keeping it together so she could finish the song.

The crowd erupted into applause when Steve uttered the iconic words "That's all, folks."

Pam threw her arms around his neck when he rejoined her and hugged him to her. "That was incredible," she said, still sputtering with laughter.

Steve hugged her back until other partygoers,

offering their congratulations on his effort, drew them apart.

They were both surprised when the grandfather clock chimed twelve.

Pam looked around her. The crowd had been thinning out for the last hour. She couldn't believe that they'd been there for more than six hours. She felt a hand on her elbow and turned to find Steve behind her.

"I'm glad to see that you haven't done a runner."

"You mean like Cinderella?"

"Exactly."

"We're practically the last ones here," Pam said.

"Have you had fun?"

"Absolutely! This is the best party I've been to in ages."

"Me, too. And we weren't with dates. Funny how that works."

"Let's get my coat, say our goodbyes to Barb and Brian, and head for home." She brought her hand to her mouth to cover a yawn.

"I'm that boring, am I?" He led her to the coat closet.

"Not at all. The day's just catching up with me."

They thanked their hosts for a fabulous evening and made their way to Steve's truck.

"Between the two of us, I'd guess we work with half of the people at the party," Steve said as he navigated the short drive to Pam's house.

"I think you're right. And I was worried I wouldn't know anybody."

"I'm not good at small talk with strangers," he said, "but I had plenty of friends in there."

"I watched you, interacting with people. These folks love you, Steve. And it was so nice of you to make a special effort with Henry Harmon. I noticed how he was sitting alone. You know, your injury forced you to lead a much different life than you'd planned, but you've made a significant impact right here in Linden Falls."

"Henry's a nice guy. And I noticed that when Ms. Cabot wasn't bustling around doing other things to help Barb, she was coming by to check on him and bring him treats every so often." He pulled into her driveway and put the car in park, hopping out to open her door for her.

"I hope you're happy here," she continued as she took his hand and stepped out of the truck.

"In Linden Falls? Yes, I am," Steve said. "After throwing myself a very long pity party, I realized I needed to focus on all the good things in my life. I've got so much more than most people ever dream of having."

They stepped onto her front porch, and she fumbled in her purse for her key.

He leaned against the doorframe, close enough for her to smell the remnants of his aftershave. She forced her mind back to her task and found her key. She put it in the lock and turned it. The door opened a crack.

She turned to him and could feel his breath on her face.

"Thank you…for the ride." She looked up at him.

He straightened and leaned close.

She closed her eyes. Was he…?

"No problem," he said, pulling himself back from her. "See you Monday morning at the gym."

Pam cleared her throat, pushed the door open, and stepped over the threshold. "Have a nice day tomorrow."

Steve turned and walked quickly back to his truck.

Pam watched until he put it in gear and began backing out of her driveway. She sighed heavily and set the security chain on her door. This hadn't been a date, she reminded herself.

Leopold appeared out of the shadows and rubbed against her legs.

Pam picked up her cat, planted a kiss on the top of his head, and got ready for bed.

CHAPTER 17

Steve stuck his head inside the trainers' break room. "I thought I saw you come in here. Do you have a minute?"

"Can it wait until tomorrow?" Pam shoved her arms into her jacket, grabbed her purse from her locker, and slammed it shut. "I need to get to Duncan's Hardware before it closes, and I'm running late."

He walked with her as she hurried to the door.

"They'll close early tomorrow for Christmas Eve. They just received my special-order farmhouse sink and restaurant-style faucet. If I pick them up now, I'll get started on the installation as soon as I'm done with work tomorrow." She pressed her nose into her elbow and sneezed loudly.

"Sure," he said, holding the door open for her. "I just want to see you before Christmas, that's all."

Pam gave him the thumbs-up sign before turning her head to sneeze again.

He watched her as she sprinted to her car. His surprise could wait until tomorrow. He'd even offer to help her with the sink and faucet. With his sister's clan out of town to visit his brother-in-law's family, he'd spend a very low-key Christmas with his parents.

Steve retreated into the gym and finished with his last two clients. He checked the next day's schedule before going home. Pam was supposed to be in by ten. He smiled to himself. The package he'd clumsily wrapped in Christmas paper sat in his locker. He hoped his small gift would bring a smile to her face.

The following morning, however, did not find Pam at the gym. Her sneezes from the day before, harbingers of a nasty head cold, had taken root overnight. With a low-grade fever, a hacking cough, and a nose that wouldn't stop running, Pam had canceled on all of her clients.

Steve swallowed his disappointment. His gift was silly, really. No big deal. He'd give it to her when she came back to the gym. He texted a message to feel better and have a merry Christmas, added a string of smiley face emojis, and pressed send.

Her response was swift but brief.

Thank you. Same to you! She appended a Christmas tree emoji.

He straightened his shoulders. He'd be done with his clients by one; then, he'd have a day and a half off in the middle of the week. He usually loved the opportunity to kick back and relax. Today should be no different. He wouldn't let sentimental feelings about being with a special someone during the holidays spoil his alone time.

Steve forced a smile onto his lips and greeted his next client as the man entered the weight room. He'd just have to wait to see Pam's reaction to his little surprise.

CHAPTER 18

*P*am claimed a spot along the wall of the Asian restaurant. Her order wasn't ready yet. The steady stream of customers in and out, picking up to-go orders, indicated that everyone else in Linden Falls was also opting for takeout food on New Year's Eve.

She was glad that she'd felt well enough to shower and wash her hair before going out to pick up her food. It had been a rough week. She'd canceled all of her training appointments and spent the prior four days in bed. She couldn't remember the last time she'd had such a solitary holiday. It felt good to get out of the house and see someone other than Leopold. Even she and her mom had only talked on the phone.

Pam flattened herself to the wall to let a woman laden with takeout bags in both arms pass by. The door opened, and her heart did a flip-flop when she saw the man entering the restaurant.

Steve stepped to the counter just as the woman operating the register held up a paper bag and called her name.

Steve turned in her direction, his face a mosaic of fatigue and sadness.

Their eyes met, and a smile changed his expression like someone had shaken an Etch A Sketch.

"She lives!" he said as she joined him at the register.

"Just barely. What a week." She handed the woman her credit card as another woman asked Steve for his name.

The woman turned to examine the tickets on the bags lined up on a long counter behind her. "This one's yours," the woman said, passing the bag across the counter to Steve as she removed the ticket.

"Put that one on my card," Pam told the woman.

"No. You don't have to do that," Steve said.

"I want to," Pam said. "I'd planned to bring you those Wishing Tree Inn muffins you love on Christmas Eve, but I couldn't get out of bed. Let me buy your dinner."

"Well...thank you."

The woman handed Pam her credit card.

Steve picked up Pam's order, together with his own, and the two headed out into the early dusk. The sky was blanketed with heavy clouds, and freezing rain had begun to fall. He walked her to her car. "I have a small gift for you."

"Really?" Pam couldn't keep the little-girl excitement out of her voice.

"I have it in my truck. I'll go get it."

The frigid rain came down harder.

Pam opened her car door. "You'll catch your death. Why don't you bring your food to my place? You can give me the gift there. We can eat and watch a game?"

"That'd be great! Or we can watch a movie."

"We'll figure it out," she said as she slipped into the driver's seat. "Now, go!"

He nodded and sprinted to his truck.

By the time they got to Pam's, the rain was coming down in sheets. Steve texted Pam to stay in her car. He had an umbrella somewhere in his truck. He'd find it and escort her to her door.

Pam shook her head. How could such a considerate guy still be single?

True to his word, Steve opened her car door, holding a large golf umbrella over her head. The takeout bags with their food were lined up on his arm.

When Pam stood, one of her feet slipped out from under her on the icy driveway. She lunged for Steve and steadied herself. As they walked to her front door, he circled her with the arm that held the umbrella aloft until she was safely inside.

Steve followed her to the kitchen and put their food on the counter. "I need to get your gift."

"I hate to send you back out in this..." she began to protest.

He held up his hand. "Be right back."

Pam busied herself setting her table and putting the takeout boxes in the center. The pungent aromas of

Mongolian beef and sweet and sour chicken made her stomach growl.

Steve returned as she was removing water bottles from the refrigerator. "It's this or cranberry juice, I'm afraid."

"Water is my drink of choice, anyway," he said. He took the bottle she handed him. "Do you want to open it?" he asked, handing her an oddly shaped package wrapped in Santa Claus paper and topped with a red bow that had seen better days. "Sorry about that," he said, pointing to the bow. "This has been riding around in my truck since before Christmas." He swayed, shifting his weight from foot to foot.

Pam felt her face flush. Steve was excited to give her this gift. "Don't be silly," she said. "It looks great." She found the fold in the wrapping and slid her finger under the taped edge, freeing it. She ripped the paper aside, and her heart caught in her throat.

She held a package of watercolor pencils, similar to the one she'd remarked on when they'd been sorting toys. This set boasted at least two dozen additional colored pencils. She looked up at him, her eyes shining. "You remembered when I said I wanted these!"

He nodded, grinning. "Did I get the right ones?"

"You most certainly did—except you got me a much bigger package." She stepped to him and drew him into a hug. "This is so thoughtful of you, Steve. I can't believe you remembered."

He relaxed into the feeling of her.

They remained in each other's arms until Steve

took a step away. "You're welcome. They're just pencils."

"Wait until you see what I can do with these pencils," Pam said. "Or at least what I hope I can do. I used to be quite good at drawing and painting. I'm way out of practice."

"I'm sure it'll come back to you. I'd like to hear about that…" he began as they sat at the kitchen table and attacked their food. When they'd finished eating, Pam walked to the counter and began rummaging through the carrier bags.

"What're you looking for?"

"Fortune cookies." She tossed one of the bags aside and picked up the other one. "There aren't any—in either of these bags!"

"What?"

"I know. I can't believe they forgot to put them in our bags."

"That's no good." He got to his feet. "I'll go back and get them."

"You'll do no such thing. It's a miserable night out there, and I'm not sending you out for some stupid fortune cookies. Thank you for offering, but I don't believe in all of that nonsense. Do you?"

He shook his head. "Shamrocks, fortune cookies, the Wishing Tree—I don't think any of them are real."

They swept the remains of their meals into the kitchen trash and settled on the sofa. They watched a football game until the third quarter, when the outcome seemed inevitable. Steve turned away from the game and insisted that she choose a movie.

She put on *The Holiday*. "I love everything about this film."

"I can see why," he said as the movie progressed. "There's lots of cool house stuff."

The clock approached midnight when the final credits filled the screen.

Steve scooted to the edge of his seat. "I'd better go."

Pam grabbed the remote and switched to a live feed from Times Square. "Let's watch the countdown," she said.

Steve settled back, and they watched the iconic "Ten... nine... eight... seven... six... five... four... three... two... one" until the ball crashed and fireworks went off.

The announcer said, "Turn to the person next to you and start the New Year with a kiss!"

Pam chuckled and leaned toward Steve, aiming for his cheek.

Steve simultaneously made the same move, aiming for her other cheek.

They each realized they were headed for the other's lips and quickly turned in the opposite direction, assuring the unintended outcome.

Their mouths met in the middle. Their breath intermingled and Pam felt the fullness of his lips. Neither of them withdrew.

Pam put her hand on Steve's chest. He covered it

with one of his own and brought his other arm around her, pulling her close.

Their lips held, each of them pressing into the other. Pam wrapped her free arm around his neck.

Steve shifted his weight, leaning her back over his arm, the urgency of his kiss increasing.

Leopold, who had spent the evening napping on the back of the sofa, opened one eye to observe the scene in front of him. He stood and stretched.

Pam clung to Steve as she lost herself in the dizzying sensations of the moment.

Leopold stared at his owner, then meowed and crouched. He launched himself into the sliver of space separating Pam and Steve, squirming to get between them.

Pam was the first to pull back. She removed her hand from Steve's neck and steered Leopold toward the edge of the sofa. The cat yowled in protest and hopped onto the floor.

Steve sat upright, breathing heavily.

Pam looked into his eyes, certain of one thing. She loved this Steve Turner.

His eyes searched her face with yearning.

She held her breath, waiting for him to kiss her again. He leaned toward her, and she shut her eyes. The next thing she knew, he was talking instead of kissing her again.

"Sorry about that," Steve said.

Her eyes shot open in disbelief.

"Really. I'm so sorry. I don't know what came over me. I guess it was all that romantic crap in *The Holiday*."

Romantic crap? Was that what he thought this was?

"I can't imagine why I did that."

Pam's body went rigid. He was saying he didn't feel anything for her. She bit her lip to keep from crying. Once again, she'd misread the situation and was getting her heart broken.

He stood abruptly and strode to the door. "I'd better go. Thank you, again, for dinner."

Pam rose and followed him. "You're welcome. Thank you for my pencils," she said in a monotone.

"See you at the gym next week."

"Sure."

He fidgeted in the doorway, avoiding eye contact. "I guess we got through another New Year's Eve without any relationship drama." He stepped out the door.

Pam shut it firmly behind him. As was his custom, Leopold emerged from the shadows.

"Men—human men—are idiots, Leopold. Complete idiots." She scooped him up and buried her now soggy face in his fur, allowing his rumbling purr to comfort her.

CHAPTER 19

"Happy New Year," Brian said, clapping Steve on the back as they entered the weight room together. "How was your Christmas?"

"Quiet. Nice. The highlight was your party."

"Glad you—and Pam—could come. You looked like you were having a wonderful time."

"We were," Steve said, handing him a weighted bar.

"Did you see her again during the holidays?"

"Yes—we were actually together on New Year's Eve."

Brian's eyebrows shot up. "You took her out on New Year's Eve? Nice going!"

"It wasn't like that. We ran into each other picking up takeout food. I had a small gift for Pam in my truck. It was pelting rain, so I went back to her place to give it to her. I ended up staying there to eat, and then we watched a football game and a movie."

Brian paused, the bar pressed over his head. "That's it?"

"What do you mean?"

"Anything romantic? I saw the two of you at our party—there's chemistry between you."

Steve hesitated.

Brian waited.

"We did kiss—at midnight."

"Yes!" Brian did two fast repetitions with the bar. "I knew it. When are you going to see her again?"

"That's just it," Steve said. "That kiss was a mistake."

"What're you talking about? Was it a bad kiss? Did she push you away?"

"It was a great kiss, but it happened by accident. We were going for each other's cheeks, but then we somehow turned into each other, and our lips met."

Brian put the bar on the floor and stood. "Doesn't sound like an accident to me. Even if it was, so what? You both enjoyed the kiss. Can't you take it from there?"

Steve's shoulders drooped. "I was worried that I'd offended her. She's become a good friend, and I didn't want to mess that up, so I apologized to her—right then and there. Told her I hadn't meant to kiss her."

Now Brian's shoulders dropped. "You didn't."

Steve looked at the floor and nodded.

"So now Pam thinks that you regret kissing her?"

"I'm afraid so."

"Have you seen her since then?"

"She's been here—at the gym—but I haven't had the chance to talk to her. I think she's avoiding me."

Brian rubbed his chin. "I think that's a good sign."

"You do?"

"I'll bet she liked that kiss as much as you did, and she's upset you said it was a mistake. If she agreed that it was a mistake, things would be business as usual for you."

"I hadn't thought of that." Steve's countenance cleared like storm clouds driven by a strong wind. "What do you think I should do...to make things right?"

"Why don't you ask her out?"

"You mean...like on a date?"

"Honestly—you young folks are as dense as a Christmas fruitcake. Yes, ask her out on a date."

"Should I talk about the kiss first?"

"No!" Brian waved his hands in front of himself. "Leave that alone. It's over and done with. Find something that you'd both enjoy and ask her to join you."

"The Home and Garden Show is next weekend," Steve said. "She's big into DIY and remodeling that new house of hers. I'm interested in that stuff, myself, and I'm sure she'd love to go."

"That's a pro move, my friend," Brian said. "It's a two-and-a-half-hour drive to Boston. That'll give you a full day together. You can get back here and take her to a lovely dinner and—"

Steve held up a hand to cut him off. "Let's see if she says yes first."

"Okay, okay. As I said, I'm sure Pam likes you. I think she'll say yes."

"From your lips to God's ears, as they say. But now that we've spent half your session talking about my issues, let's get back to business."

※》》》

STEVE CAUGHT sight of Pam speed walking to the exit. He'd been trying to flag her down in the hallway or catch her in the trainers' break room for the past week —with no luck. He sprinted through the lobby and caught up to her as she reached for the long metal bar to open the door.

"Hey," he said, slightly breathless. "I haven't seen you since...all week."

"I've been crazy busy, haven't you? All those new clients who've made resolutions to get in shape this year."

Steve laughed. "January is my busiest month." He stopped, suddenly tongue-tied.

"Well...I'd better go," Pam said, pushing on the metal bar.

"I was wondering if you'd like to go to the Boston Home and Garden Show with me next Sunday," he blurted out. "I know you're fixing up your place. It's fun to see all the new stuff that's available."

Pam stepped back from the door. She'd been contemplating doing just that.

"I'd pick you up early. We could have breakfast on

the way and be there when the doors open. We can spend all day—or not. We'll leave when you're ready to go."

Pam tilted her face to his. "I'm surprised you're interested in this."

"I've been a huge fan of *This Old House* for years. Don't tell anyone"—he leaned close to her—"but I've been known to watch HGTV, too."

She could smell a whiff of his aftershave. Her stomach did a flip-flop. She'd be spending five hours in a car, close enough to touch him, and the rest of the day at his side. His offer was made out of friendship, but her feelings for him were more than friendly. All that time with him would only intensify those feelings. She'd end up being even sadder than she already was. Until she could move him back into the friend zone, she needed to stay away from him.

She turned abruptly to the door. "That's okay—I think I'll pass on it this year. You go and have a good time."

"Sure...well...see you around."

She didn't see his eyes dull or his lips settle in a hard line.

Pam stepped out into the frigid January afternoon. Her eyes stung—whether from the cold or her rising tears, she didn't know.

CHAPTER 20

"*I*'m surprised you didn't go," Barb said as she finished her workout. "I thought you got a ton of great ideas from the Home and Garden Show last year."

"I was going to but changed my mind."

"Oh?"

Pam inhaled slowly through her nose. "To be honest, Steve invited me, and I said no."

"Why? I think every single woman in this place"— she swung her arm in an arc around herself—"would jump at the chance to spend a day with him. He's the most eligible bachelor in town."

Pam looked at Barb, and her eyes telegraphed pain. "That's just it. I'm one of those women."

"What's wrong with that?"

"He doesn't feel that way about me. He's made it abundantly clear that he doesn't want a romantic relationship and that we're just friends."

"You don't know that."

"I do." Pam told Barb about the New Year's Eve kiss and Steve's apology.

"For crying out loud." Barb sighed in exasperation. "He asked you to the Home and Garden Show, didn't he?"

"Yes—but just as a friend. I'm sure of it."

"I don't think so, honey. If you felt that kind of spark from your kiss, I'm sure it affected Steve the same way. That's why he asked you out."

"You mean that?"

"Yes. I can still picture both of you at our party. You're smitten with each other, and you're the only ones who don't know it."

Pam slumped against the wall and brought her hands to her temples. "Now what? How can I fix this?"

"Since he made the last move—which you rejected —it's time for you to approach him."

"What if we're wrong, and he's not interested?"

"Then he'll say no, and you'll have your answer. And don't tell me you don't want to risk getting hurt. You're already hurting. Better to get the answer, one way or another."

Pam nodded. "Makes sense. I know just what I'll say to him."

"You'll be a modern woman and ask him out?"

"I will. Thanks for the push."

Barb grinned. "That's what friends are for. Unless I miss my bet, he's crazy about you."

※》》

PAM SEARCHED every nook and cranny of Linden Falls Fitness—except the men's locker room. When she didn't find Steve, she sprinted around the parking lot. His car wasn't there. He must have finished his Friday sessions early and left for the weekend.

The game was Sunday afternoon. She'd wanted to ask him in person—to gauge his reaction as she went along. Pam pursed her lips. She'd just have to invite him in a text. Barb was right—she had to find out if he was interested in her—*in that way*—or not.

She pulled out her phone, typing, backspacing, and typing some more until she was satisfied with her message.

Our favorite teams are playing each other on Sunday afternoon. I'm making a big pot of chili, jalapeño cornbread, and s'mores cookies for dessert. Care (dare) to join me?

She added a smiley face emoji and a football emoji and pressed send.

She replaced her phone in her locker and hurried to her last training session of the week.

By the time she and her client had finished, she was more than a little anxious to see if Steve had responded. Unfortunately, the young mother was working hard to lose her baby weight and, as usual, had nutrition questions for Pam. She usually enjoyed this coaching aspect of her job, but tonight she could barely mask her impatience.

When the woman thanked her for her time and said

goodbye, it had been more than an hour since Pam had sent her message.

She checked her phone as soon as she fished it out of her purse. The cracked mirror on the inside of her locker door perfectly reflected her shattered hopes. His response had been brief and definitive.

Already have other plans. Thanks. Have a nice weekend.

She snatched her purse and jacket from their hook and slammed her locker shut. She had her answer— Steve wasn't interested in her. She'd been a fool to think otherwise.

She stuffed her hands into her pockets and strode out to her car in a huff. Maybe it was better this way. Instead of wasting time in the kitchen, cooking and baking cookies, she'd retile her shower. At least her efforts were sure to result in something she'd enjoy for years.

CHAPTER 21

Neva bent to examine the fabric swatches spread out on the long table in the tea room. She looked at Irene. "I love these! Any one of them would be beautiful in here. Which one do you like best?"

Irene stepped back and narrowed her eyes, shifting them from the fabrics to the wallpaper and drapes and back again. "I think the simpler, the better." She picked up a red-and-white-striped swatch. Small bouquets of pink flowers, tied with red ribbons, were scattered at irregular intervals across the fabric. "This would be lovely for both the aprons and tablecloths." She pointed to another sample: a lush floral print in shades of pink ranging from blush to deep magenta, accented by leaves in every shade of green. "We could make a long cloth out of this to dress the service table." She laid the striped sample on top of the rich floral.

"They look wonderful together. Let's do it!"

"It'll be stunning, and these fabrics aren't limited to Valentine's Day. You'll be able to use them again and again."

"I'd love that," Neva said. "If this series of teas during the week before Valentine's Day is popular, Janie is planning to hold them every month."

"I'm sure they will be. Afternoon Book Club Tea is a genius idea."

"I hope so. Town Square Books came up with it. They're picking a book, and the author will make a presentation at each of the teas and lead a discussion on their book."

"I'm coming to the tea on Tuesday of that week. I just bought the book and can't wait to start it."

"Be sure to bring your copy to the tea. The author will sign it, and you'll be able to buy her other books if you like her writing."

"Sounds like a win-win for the bookstore, the author, and you. I love that."

"Okay. Decision made." Neva ran her hand across the fabrics they'd selected. "Speaking of Valentine's Day, how's Pam doing in the dating world?"

Irene began folding the samples and stacking them on the table. "Not well, I'm afraid. She had three bad dates from the online service—to be honest, they were terrible—and gave up."

"Anyone else she might be interested in?"

"I thought she and Steve might have something going. They saw a lot of each other during the toy drive, and she talked about him nonstop. I was getting my hopes up—I think they're perfect for each other..."

"I do, too," Neva said, holding Irene's satchel open as Irene slid the samples inside.

"But something happened—over New Year's—I think."

"Any idea what?"

Irene pursed her lips and shook her head. "No idea. I've tried to wheedle it out of Pam, but she doesn't want to talk about it. All she ever says is that she's perfectly happy on her own, and she wants to work on her house."

The two women's eyes locked.

"I don't believe her, do you?" Neva asked.

"Nope."

"Those two belong together."

"Without a doubt. I wish I could make it happen."

"Like setting them up on a blind date?"

Irene chuckled. "Wouldn't that be great? Except they already know each other."

"So? They can still meet on a blind date."

"That's the other thing. She's taken a no-dating pledge—with Steve, of all people."

Neva leaned against the window frame and gazed across the street to where the Wishing Tree stood in the cold sunshine. Its branches were bare, except for a handful of wishes that fluttered in the light breeze.

"I can't figure out how to get through to her."

"There's got to be a way. I'll bet Barb and Brian could think of something."

Irene cocked her head to one side. "What do they have to do with this?"

Neva's brows furrowed. "You know I never divulge anyone's wish."

"I do. As the official keeper of wishes, your reputation for confidentiality is legendary."

"Just this once, I think I can make an exception."

Irene leaned toward Neva. A smile washed over Irene's lips as she listened to Neva's whispered description of Barb's wish. "I had no idea she'd wished for the same thing we have. I think you're right—Barb and Brian can set them up on a blind date. Barb is Pam's favorite client—she'd do anything for her."

"Brian has worked with Steve for years. He'll be able to talk Steve into it if anybody can. I'll call Barb," Neva said. "Let's try to get Pam and Steve here for dinner on Valentine's Day."

Irene clasped her hands together. "Wouldn't that be wonderful!"

The women walked to the foyer. Neva opened the front door. A gentle breeze stirred the limbs of the Wishing Tree, which now appeared to be saluting them.

Neva and Irene turned to each other, wide-eyed, then burst out laughing.

"I think the Wishing Tree approves of our plan, too," Neva said.

"Based on that, I know we won't fail." Irene hugged Neva quickly and was on her way.

CHAPTER 22

*P*am opened the trainers' break room door and was relieved to find herself alone. She hadn't seen Steve since they had passed each other in the weight room at lunchtime. Maybe he'd gone home early.

She grabbed her jacket and surveyed the hallway in front of her. No Steve. The last thing she wanted to do was run into him. It was Valentine's Day, and she was headed home to get ready for her blind date.

Pam sped across the lobby and hit the metal bar on the entry door at a trot. She must have been out of her mind to promise that she would let Barb fix her up with "the perfect guy" if Barb lost five pounds in three weeks. In truth, Barb had been struggling to lose those last five pounds for months. Pam had assumed she'd never have to live up to her end of the bargain.

She walked up to her car, reached for her purse, and

cursed. She'd left it in her locker. Where was her mind these days? Now she'd have to go back to get it.

Pam straightened her shoulders and took a deep breath. Now there was another chance she'd run into Steve and she hated the prospect. Hadn't they both commiserated just yesterday about how ridiculous Valentine's Day was? What a boatload of commercialized, sentimental nonsense? They'd even reiterated their no-dating pledge to each other. She'd felt awful about lying, but she didn't want to confess to having a date tonight.

She hurried into the gym and retrieved her purse without seeing Steve. Instead of heading out the main entrance, she took the rarely used back stairs, which led to an exit on the far side of the building. She'd have to walk around the building on an uneven gravel walkway to return to the parking lot, but the obscure route was worth it.

The exit door was heavy and stuck when she pushed it. She put her shoulder against the door and put her weight into it. The door gave way, and she stumbled as she stepped outside. A familiar pair of hands grabbed her shoulders to steady her.

"Steve," she said, trying to regain her balance and her composure.

"Hi," he said. "Why are you using the back stairs?"

"I do…sometimes," she said. "Why're you here?"

"I parked at the curb." He pointed to his truck behind him. "I have something to bring out—from my locker."

"Do you need help with it? It must be heavy if you needed to park close."

"No. I've got it."

"Okay. Good."

"Are you done for the day? Isn't it kind of early?"

"I marked myself out this afternoon." She bit her lip. "I'm going to the book club tea at the Wishing Tree Inn." She hoped he couldn't tell that she was lying. Her mother had gone and had told her all about it, so she could cover for herself if he asked her about it later. She wasn't going to tell him that she was going home to wash her hair and do her makeup for a blind date.

Steve took a step back. He'd be at the Wishing Tree Inn later that evening for his Valentine's Day blind date. He should never have bet on that game with Brian. Steve's team had been favored to win by seventeen points. They'd lost, and now, here he was, trying to sneak in via the back stairs to retrieve the bouquet he'd stored in his locker since he'd picked up the flowers at lunchtime. He didn't know why he'd bought them anyway—this date was certain to end in disappointment like all the others. Still, he'd feel like a heel not to show up with flowers on Valentine's Day.

"Steve? Are you okay?"

Steve snapped his attention back to Pam.

"Sure. Yes. I'm just fine. I'd better let you go. You don't want to be late for your...what was it? Tea?"

Pam swallowed hard and nodded. "See you tomorrow."

"You bet," Steve said, bounding up the stairs.

>))))

EVEN WITH THE help of Janie and the girls, Neva had been on her feet since dawn. The Valentine's Book Club Teas had been a rousing success, and they were fully booked for dinner that night. With any luck, this would be her biggest revenue day since she'd taken over the inn.

She checked her watch. She had enough time to sit down with a cup of tea before the dinner crowd arrived, or she could take care of the errand she'd wanted to do all day. There wasn't time for her to do both.

Neva pulled her coat around her shoulders and retrieved the five wishes from the top drawer of her desk, where they'd been waiting for just this moment for weeks. She set out for the square. It was time for these special wishes—united in their desire for the same outcome—to return to the magical tree.

CHAPTER 23

Steve opened the door to the Wishing Tree Inn and slipped inside. He scanned the foyer and looked toward the tea room on the right.

The overhead lights had been turned down in the room. The tables were covered in starched linen cloths. Nosegays of roses and baby's breath sat in the middle of each table, flanked by votive candles. The flickering light glinted on silver flatware and crystal glasses. Classic love songs from the Sinatra era played in the background.

Steve released the breath he'd been holding. The room was set for dinner. He wouldn't bump into Pam, still enjoying her tea.

He approached the hostess stand and gave his name to a young girl who looked barely old enough to work but, judging by her expression, took her job very seri-ously. "I believe you have a reservation for two at seven o'clock. I know I'm early, but I'd like to be seated."

"Certainly," the girl said, grabbing two printed paper menus. "My name is Breeze and if you follow me, I'll take you to your table."

She led Steve to a spot by the window overlooking the square.

He sat with his back to the window so that he could watch people coming and going in the dining room.

"Will this be all right?" Breeze asked, handing him a menu and putting the other menu down at the place setting across from him.

"Perfect." He set the bouquet of yellow roses, tipped with pink, on the table.

"Those are lovely," she said.

"I have a friend who likes them," he said, remembering that Pam had shown him a picture of a similar rose she'd special- ordered to plant in her yard. There had been one bouquet of these roses at Petals when he'd walked in at lunchtime, and he'd immediately snatched it up.

"Who are you waiting for?" Breeze asked. "So I can bring her over to the table."

"Uh...well..." Steve cleared his throat. "I'm not too sure."

Her eyebrows shot up, but she didn't comment.

"It's a blind date."

Breeze grinned. "How nice." She pointed to the flowers. "That's a thoughtful touch."

"Thank you," he replied as she turned and went back to her station.

Steve spent the next ten minutes looking from his

watch to the hostess station and back again. Brian hadn't given him any sort of physical description of the woman he'd be meeting—other than that she was stunning and had a lot in common with Steve.

Steve had taken a sip of his water when a familiar figure walked to the hostess stand. He could only see her in profile, but he'd know her anywhere.

Pam had abandoned her usual ponytail, and her long hair hung in soft curls that caressed her shoulders. The hostess said something that made her laugh, and her smile lit up the room. She removed her coat and folded it over her arm.

Steve thought about changing seats and slipping into the chair opposite him, putting his back to the dining room, but decided against it. The room was small, and at some point, they'd see each other.

Breeze turned and moved toward the dining room.

Pam followed.

Steve wanted to avert his eyes but couldn't. Pam looked radiant in a shimmering silver sheath that hugged her well-toned curves.

They were headed directly toward him. He swallowed hard as Breeze swept her arm to one side, gesturing to Steve's table.

Pam's eyes flew open when she recognized Steve. Their gazes met, and they stared at each other until they both burst out laughing. Steve rose and held her chair for Pam, both of them gasping for air as the hilarity continued.

"You two know each other?" Breeze asked.

All either of them could do was nod.

"Your waitress will be right over," she said. "Enjoy your evening."

"I guess we're both busted," Pam said.

"That we are." Steve regained control of his breathing. "You look absolutely stunning." His voice was husky and his eyes telegraphed the truth of his words.

Pam blushed. "Thank you. You're looking very handsome, yourself."

Steve handed her the bouquet. "These are for you."

Pam brought them to her nose and inhaled their fragrance. "They're gorgeous. I planted six bushes of roses like these along the side of my house. They're my favorite."

"I remember you mentioned that."

"Wait—did you know I'd be your blind date?"

"No. Brian never breathed a word of their plan. I went to Petals this morning, and this bouquet stood out above all the rest. The fact that you love them must have been planted in my subconscious."

Pam beamed at him. "Thank you."

"You're welcome."

They considered each other across the table.

Steve was the first to speak again. "I'm thrilled you're here—that my date is you, Pam."

"I'm happy about it, too."

"I've been thinking about you nonstop since New Year's Eve." He leaned across the table. "No, since well before that. I was jealous about all of your blind dates from that online service."

"But that mistaken New Year's Eve kiss—"

"That was no mistake," Steve interrupted her.

"Then why did you say that it was?"

"I was afraid I'd tricked you into it—that you'd be mad at me. I didn't want to lose your friendship."

"I wasn't feeling that way at all. I loved that kiss."

"That's what Brian said." Steve grinned sheepishly. "He convinced me to try again—with that invitation to the Home and Garden Show."

Pam put her hand to her head. "Oh, boy."

"You turned me down flat."

"I thought you wanted to keep us firmly in the friend zone. I had feelings for you and thought that spending an entire day with you would only make me miserable."

Steve blew out a breath.

"Barb told me that I was wrong—that you did like me—so I invited you over for chili and to watch the game."

"And I said no because I thought sitting on that sofa, close enough to kiss you, would be torture."

"I'll bet there's some great Shakespearean quote that would describe us, but I can't think what it would be."

Steve chuckled and took her hands in his. "I'm glad we're here, together, right now."

"Me, too," Pam said. "And we can throw the no-dating pledge out the window."

He shook his head. "Let's modify it. No dating anyone except each other."

"Are you asking me to go steady?" Pam joked.

"I'm asking for more than that," he replied. Steve brought his hand to her face and traced her cheek with his thumb. His eyes were reservoirs of desire. Pam turned her lips into his hand and kissed his palm. Steve hooked his index finger under her chin, drawing her toward him as he leaned across the table and brought his lips to hers.

The insistence of his mouth on hers sent shivers to Pam's toes. She smelled his aftershave above the aroma of the roses. Steve continued pressing his mouth against hers.

They were in a public place—she should pull back from him. The thought soon fled as her senses filled with the feel and smell of him.

Steve reached his other arm toward her. He was drawing her closer when his elbow collided with her water glass. The glass teetered, then tipped over onto the tabletop, sending a rivulet of water across the surface and onto the floor.

The icy droplets splashing onto her knee made Pam jump.

The spell of their kiss broken, Steve snatched his napkin off of his lap and placed it over the spill. Pam followed suit with her napkin. Steve clasped her hand, and they looked from the soggy mess on the table into each other's eyes. Then, for the second time that evening, they both burst out laughing.

"I COULDN'T EAT ANOTHER BITE," Pam said, sinking against the back of her chair. "That chocolate soufflé was incredible. Worth every calorie."

"Would you like another refill on your coffee?" Steve asked.

"I'll be up half the night as it is," Pam said. "It's almost eleven, and we both have clients at five thirty tomorrow morning."

"Are you saying you think we should call it a night?"

"As much as I hate this to end, yes."

Steve arched an eyebrow. "Let's just postpone the end of this date until Saturday. Are you free?"

"I am."

"Then Saturday night it is. I'll pick you up at six, and we can kick this off old-school style with dinner and a movie."

"I'd love that."

Steve signaled to their waitress, using his hand to make a check sign.

Neva intercepted the young woman on her way to their table. She approached them, smiling broadly. "It's so good to see the two of you together. Did you enjoy yourselves?"

"The food was fabulous," Steve said. "I don't think I've ever had a better meal."

"I'm delighted to hear that. I'll be sure to tell Carly —she spent weeks working on this menu and she's in the kitchen waiting on pins and needles to see how it went over."

"Please tell her that chocolate soufflé was amazing," Pam said.

"Would you mind asking our waitress to bring our check? We hate to leave, but we both have clients early tomorrow."

"Oh...I thought you knew. Your bill has already been paid."

Steve swept his gaze around the almost- deserted room. "By whom?"

Neva's eyes sparkled. "Can't you guess?"

"Brian and Barb?" Steve asked.

"Of course. They were so tickled to be able to set you up."

"They're so sweet," Pam said.

Neva crossed her arms over her chest. "A lot of people were rooting for you to get together." She stepped around the table and parted the window blinds, pointing to the Wishing Tree.

Steve and Pam both craned their necks to see what she was pointing at. The Wishing Tree stood in the moonlight, with five wishes twisting and turning in the breeze.

"Why don't you wander over there and read those wishes hanging on the tree?"

"I've never believed in all that Wishing Tree nonsense," Steve began before Neva held up her hand to cut him off.

"Let's go take a look," Pam said. She felt the same way Steve did about the silly, sentimental tree, but she wanted to placate Neva. She rose from her chair and turned to Neva, sweeping her into a hug. "Thank you for such a wonderful dinner."

Neva gave her a quick kiss on the cheek. "You'd better go if you have to be up so early."

Steve helped Pam on with her coat. She cradled her bouquet of roses in her arms. Steve put his hand in the small of her back, and they walked across the street, into the square, and made their way to the Wishing Tree.

Steve reached up and read each of the five wishes aloud.

"The one that wants her daughter and 'Steve' to fall in love is from my mother," Pam said, standing on tiptoes to read the wish. "That's her handwriting."

Steve pointed to two other papers. "These two look like they were written by the same person."

"Barb?" Pam guessed.

"I'd say so." Steve drew Pam to him. "One of those wishes was written by me—years ago—when you were my best friend's kid sister. I had a crush on you even then."

Pam tilted her chin to look at him. "Then that accounts for all the wishes. I wrote the remaining one when I first started working at the gym. I thought my brother's annoying friend had grown up into a kind and handsome man."

The wind scuttled clouds across the sky, and a full moon illuminated the Wishing Tree.

Pam laid a hand on its massive trunk. "You do grant wishes," she said softly. "I'm sorry I ever doubted you."

She looked up at Steve. "Do you believe in the magic of this tree?"

Steve swept her into his embrace. "When I'm with you, I feel like everything is magical."

Pam slipped her arms around his neck and pressed her body into his.

Their lips met, and their kiss voiced the longing and love they'd harbored for each other since they'd hung their wishes on the tree.

A cloud blew in front of the moon, plunging them into darkness.

Neva stood in the window across the street, her arms folded across her chest, watching the scene unfold under the tree. She hugged herself and sent up a prayer of thanks, then turned out the porch light and retreated to her bedroom, secure in the knowledge that the Wishing Tree had worked its magic.

THE END

EPILOGUE

When morning came, Neva was up with the roosters—if she'd had any—and so very relieved that the hustle and bustle of Valentine's Day was over and now all she had to do was help Janie with the morning dishes, check out her last guests from the weekend, and then she would have Monday all day to herself.

Well, almost to herself.

She smiled as she sunk her hands into the sudsy water at the sink and the heat rushed to her cheeks when she thought of Henry. They planned to sneak off early in the morning when the temperatures were the coolest and the town was the quietest and hike up to Linden Falls. The last time either of them had been there was when they were teenagers and had skipped school one afternoon to go there together. She blushed further when she remembered the stolen kisses they'd shared out on the biggest rock.

Today there'd be no kisses, especially not like the one she'd spied Steve and Pam sharing the night before. Lordy… Greta, Henry's late wife, hadn't been gone long enough to even consider any of that nonsense, and after all, Henry was just her friend. She needed to get any silly notions out of her head and stop walking on clouds when she thought of him.

Her life was fuller now than it had ever been. What with Janie and the girls being there full-time, with plans to never leave (hopefully), how could Neva even think of asking for more?

"Ms. Cabot!"

Startled out of her daydream, Neva turned just in time to ready herself for the launch of a little boy's arms thrown around her waist.

"Thank you for making me chocolate chip pancakes!" he cried out. "And for the caramel apple last night and telling us about the corn maze. We had so much fun and I got to ride in the hay wagon. I don't want to leave but I have sailing class next week. Can we come back again?"

She laughed as he said all of that with his face muffled into her apron. Despite her wet hands, she clutched him to her as hard as she dared, trying to fill him with enough love to last him the ride home.

"Oh, Cameron. You are so welcome for all of it. You've been a total joy, and yes, I really do hope you come back and visit us here at the inn again. I know Myster really took a liking to you and would love to see you again."

"He took my lucky rabbit's foot!" Cameron said, backing up to look incredulously at Neva. "Stole it right out from under my pillow!"

Neva chuckled. "He sure did. That means he likes you. But we found it, didn't we? Ruined that old cat's plans to give it to his girlfriend, we did."

Cameron narrowed his eyes. "Is that really his girlfriend?"

She nodded. "It sure is. Myster and Charm have been courting for years now, and he's always trying to find her something shiny to stay in her favor."

Cameron looked confused at her choice of words.

"Cameron? Are you in there?"

They both turned.

"He's right here, Mr. Winters. Giving me a last goodbye," Neva said.

"Please, call me Mark," he said. "I feel like we're almost family now. You've been so kind and I'll be recommending this place to everyone at home. We've had a wonderful time. It was a weekend well worth the drive."

Neva beamed. It tickled her pink when her guests left happy.

"And I paid our bill online, so we're good to go. The car's all packed up and all I need now is my little co-pilot," Mark said. "Say goodbye, Cameron. We have a long day ahead of us."

Cameron gave her one final hug and then Neva walked them out. She watched wistfully as the car pulled away from the curb. The boy either hid his feelings well or was surprisingly well adjusted, considering all he'd been through.

Nothing made Neva sadder than knowing a child had suffered. She hoped with all she had that Cameron would be blessed for the rest of his life, and never have to go through heartache again, though she knew that was probably wishful thinking. Life was a series of challenges, and nobody got through it without their share.

She went to the stairs, climbing them slowly as to not upset her left knee and have it harping at her all day long.

These days the ornate staircase she once looked at so lovingly was now her nemesis, but she liked to get a peek at the rooms after the guests departed so she could plan how much time would be needed to turn them around for the next ones.

She told her knee to behave, that the stairs were just a warm-up to the plans for the next morning, and those were definitely not to be trifled with.

Mark and Cameron had stayed in the Jungle Book room. She'd actually had to do a lot of switching people around to make it happen, but after she'd learned a bit about the two of them, she had wanted the little boy's stay to be the best it could be.

She peeked into the room and was pleasantly surprised to see how neat they'd left it. They had stripped the bedding and tied it all into a neat bundle and laid it next to the bed. There wasn't a slip of trash or food wrappings to be found, and not a stray crumb from the many snacks she'd sent to their room over the last few days.

Now this is how to bring up a child, she thought, thinking of what a great example Mark was to the lad. And Cameron was going to need that in his life, for one day when he was no longer looking out of little boy eyes, and the reality of his past came crashing down around him, having a strong male figure to turn to might just save him from sinking too deep into the why and how of who he was and what he'd lost.

As she turned to go, she saw something blue through the crack of the nightstand drawer. She hurried over to open it and was alarmed to see it was a wallet with an airplane embroidered across the top. Thankful it obviously didn't belong to an adult, Neva tucked it into the pocket of her apron and started back downstairs.

With the change in routine, something told her that the inn was working its magic and the wallet had something to do with it. If Cameron had left it behind, whether on purpose or on accident, who was she to mess with destiny?

Now she just needed to be patient and see how it all played out.

NEVA IS ABSOLUTELY right and something is always happening when it comes to the magic of Linden Falls, the Wishing Tree, and the old inn. Cameron's wallet might seem like a little thing, but it will play a big part in a story of longing, loving, and healing in *A Parade of Wishes*, the next book in the Wishing Tree series, by Camille Di Maio.

﹥﹥﹥

Don't miss any books in the Wishing Tree series:

★ **Don't miss a Wishing Tree book!** ★
Book 1: The Wishing Tree – prologue book
Book 2: I Wish.. by Amanda Prowse
Book 3: Wish You Were Here by Kay Bratt
Book 4: Wish Again by Tammy L. Grace
Book 5: Workout Wishes & Valentine Kisses by
Barbara Hinske
Book 6: A Parade of Wishes by Camille Di Maio
Book 7: Careful What You Wish by Ashley Farley
Book 8: Gone Wishing by Jessie Newton
Book 9: Wishful Thinking by Kay Bratt
Book 10: Overdue Wishes by Tammy L. Grace
Book 11: A Whole Heap of Wishes by Amanda Prowse
Book 12: Wishes of Home by Barbara Hinske
Book 13: Wishful Witness by Tonya Kappes

WE ALSO INVITE you to join us in our My Book Friends group on Facebook. It's a great place to chat about all things bookish and learn more about our founding authors.

FROM THE AUTHOR

Thank you for reading the fifth book in THE WISHING TREE SERIES. I had such fun creating this world with my author friends from My Book Friends, and I hope you'll read all the books in the series. They're wonderful stories centered around a special tree in Linden Falls. If you enjoyed this story, I also hope you'll explore more of my work. You can find all my books on Amazon.

If you enjoy women's fiction, you'll want to try my bestselling ROSEMONT SERIES, filled with stories of friendship, family, romance, stately homes, and dogs—with a dash of mystery, thriller, and suspense.

My acclaimed GUIDING EMILY SERIES chronicles the life of a young woman who loses her eyesight on her honeymoon and reclaims her independence with the help of her guide dog, proving that *sometimes the perfect partner has four paws.*

If you enjoy holiday stories, be sure to check out THE CHRISTMAS CLUB (adapted for the Hallmark Channel in 2019) and PAWS & PASTRIES. They're Christmas stories of hope, friendship, and family.

If you're a fan of mysteries, look for the novels in my "WHO'S THERE?!" collection.

I hope you'll connect with me on social media. You can find me on Facebook, where I have a page and a special group for my readers, and follow me on Amazon, Goodreads, and BookBub so you'll know when I have a new release or a deal. You can also sign up for my newsletter at this link: https://barbarahinske.com/newsletter/

If you enjoyed this book or any of my other books, I'd be grateful if you took a few minutes to leave a short review on Amazon, BookBub, or Goodreads. Just a few lines would be great. Reviews are the best gift an author can receive. They encourage us when they're good, help us improve our next book when they're not, and help other readers make informed choices when purchasing books. Reviews keep the Amazon algorithms humming and are the most helpful aide in selling books! Thank you.

To post a review on Amazon:

1. Go to the product detail page for Workout Wishes & Valentine Kisses on Amazon.com.
2. Click "Write a customer review" in the Customer Reviews section.

3. Write your review and click Submit.

In gratitude,
Barbara Hinske

ABOUT THE AUTHOR

BARBARA HINSKE recently left the practice of law to pursue her writing career full time. Her novella *The Christmas Club* has been made into a Hallmark Channel Christmas movie of the same name (2019), and she feels like she's living the dream. She is extremely grateful to her readers! She inherited the writing gene from her father, who wrote mysteries when he retired and told her a story every night of her childhood. She and her husband share their own Rosemont with two adorable and spoiled dogs. The historic house keeps her husband busy with repair projects and her happily decorating, entertaining, and gardening. She also spends a lot of time baking and—as a result—dieting.

I'd Love to Hear from You! Connect with Me Online:
Sign up for my newsletter at
BarbaraHinske.com to receive your Free Gift,
plus Inside Scoops and Bedtime Stories.
Search for **Barbara Hinske on YouTube**
for tours inside my own historic home plus tips
and tricks for busy women!
Find photos of fictional Rosemont and Westbury,

adorable dogs, and things related to my books at
Pinterest.com/BarbaraHinske.
Email me at **bhinske@gmail.com** or find me at

facebook.com/BHinske

twitter.com/BarbaraHinske

instagram.com/barbarahinskeauthor

goodreads.com/Barbara_Hinske

tiktok.com/@barbarahinske

Printed in Great Britain
by Amazon